LET'S PRETEND

RIVER LAURENT

Let's Pretend

978-1-911608-33-2

ACKNOWLEDGMENTS

Thank You

Leanore Elliott
Brittany Urbaniak

SYNOPSIS

I've always had a thing for Scarlett Johnson. She has the cutest butt around town and that mouth. What I could do with that mouth! But she has always been out of bounds. She's the daughter of a man respected a great deal, but now he's dead and he has drawn up his will in such a way that his daughter needs me to marry her.

She wants it to be a pretend marriage, but I'm not known as the great big white shark in the circles I move in, for nothing. I tell her nothing is for nothing. The deal has to work both ways. She gets something and I get something.

It kills her to do it, but she agrees.

Well, well, well...Scarlett Johnson

CHAPTER 1

SCARLETT

"**W**hat?" I gasp in shock.

"I don't believe it," my younger sister blurts out.

Ernest, my father's attorney squirms slightly in his chair and pats his slightly askew-whiff hair piece. He's worked for us for so long he almost feels like part of the family. If there were anyone I would trust, it would be this man, for sure. For certain.

"It cannot be. My father would never do something like *this*. There must be some mistake," I whisper.

Ernest shakes his head.

"Are you sure? Let me see the will," Lori demands.

"I'm very sorry Scarlett and Lori, but there is no mistake," he says quietly, handing her the sheaf of papers. "I drew up this will, your father read, then signed it in front of me. This is what your father wanted."

Lori freezes beside me, and I know exactly what's running

through her head. The conversation we had with our mother right before she left us for good.

"Can I just ask you one thing?" Mom whispered, as we sat by her bed. By this point, the notion of curing her had long been abandoned, and the best we could hope for was she would be comfortable in her final few days on this Earth.

"Anything you want," I promised, and I meant it. There wasn't a thing in the world I wouldn't have done for her.

"I want you to make sure that this house stays in our family," she replied, grasping my wrist weakly in her wasted claw-like hand. "This house has a heart and a soul. The walls keep the memories of our ancestors. I grew up here, my grandmother and mother grew up here, you and Lori grew up here...it must never end up anywhere, but your hands. You are my oldest. I entrust it to you as my mother entrusted it to me. Do you promise to take care of it until you can pass it on to your heir?"

"Of course!" I exclaimed.

At that time, I hadn't even considered the idea of our home belonging to anyone else, but our family for as long as our blood flowed. How could it be? It was ours. I wanted to raise my own children here, along with Lori's brood, whenever she had them. I would have given up my life to keep my promise. But now, here I was, hearing that it is going to be ripped away from me. From us.

That Victoria is going to walk away with my mother's beloved home.

"But he wouldn't have left Wotton Hall to her!" my sister, Lori cries out. "He knew she hates it. She called it a mausoleum right to his face." She flung her hand in the direction where my stepmother is sitting, dressed from head to toe in black, milking her widowhood as if she truly is mourning.

Ernest looks at my sister and me sadly. "I'm sorry. There is nothing I can do. Your father *did* leave the Wotton Hall, the grounds, and the woods around it, to Victoria."

I sag with disbelief and confusion. How could it be? My father promised me he would leave the house to me. He knew what it meant to me. It was my mother's dying wish for me to have the house. She only left it to him temporarily to take advantage of some tax avoidance scheme his accountant had devised. He swore to her that he would pass the house to me on his death. I was there when he told her that. With tears streaming down his face, he'd promised her he would.

Tears start clogging my own throat. My father's betrayal is impossible for me to accept, or even comprehend. I was the only one present that night when he drew his last breath. He held my hand and said, "*I love you, Scarlett my darling. You are my first born and have always been my favorite. I have set it up so that you will be safe from this cruel world.*"

Then he goes and does this!

"Don't worry, you won't be homeless," Ernest says in his most comforting voice. "Your father has made provisions for both of you to live in his London apartment."

"Right, I've had enough of this nonsense," Victoria speaks up, her voice full of irritation. "What else has he left for me?"

"I'm afraid there is nothing else for you except the house and your monthly allowance that will continue to be paid to you until your dying day," Ernest says coldly.

"That's it?" she screeches. "That's what the old fool left for me?"

"That's it," Ernest says tightly.

"What about the business? The ancestral jewelry, the house in Paris and Bahamas?" she demands, her face twisting with anger.

Ernest's lips went thin. "That is for his daughters. It may surprise you to know that I believe your monthly allowance is actually too generous."

"You call that pittance, generous?" she asks scornfully. "Well, then you don't know what I've had to do for it. The stingy, decrepit bastard. I had to suck his shriveled coc—"

I see red. Without even realizing it, I jump out of my chair and streak across the room. The sound of my hand connecting with Victoria's cheek reverberates around our stunned figures.

Victoria holds her cheek and glares at me with pure hatred, but she does not dare retaliate. She can see that she has pushed me beyond civilized limits.

For the first time during this will reading, Lori smiles.

I'm ready to claw her eyes out. "Get out," I snarl. "Get out. You're a vile, disrespectful bitch. Why my father ever married a conniving gold digger like you, I'll never know."

She smiles suddenly. "It's not actually, a secret, you know. Nobody can suck dick like me. I'm sure I could give you a lesson or two about that. You look like you need it."

"You are disgusting!" Lori yells.

"Get out," I grit through clenched teeth.

"Yes, I'm going, but let me tell you my first order of business is to sell this damn place, so I'll expect you to move both your snooty asses out of my property by the end of the week," she says with a sneer before turning on her heels and walking out of the door.

CHAPTER 2

SCARLETT

I'm stunned. I can't even think straight anymore. I can feel my breath coming out of me shallow and fast.

My sister comes over to me. "Calm down, Scarlett. She's gone now."

I clasp my sister's hand tightly, then I turn to Ernest, my voice shaking with emotion as I speak, "Can I instruct you to immediately buy the house off her?"

Ernest shakes his head. "Unfortunately, no."

My eyes narrow at him.

"Why not?" Lori asks.

"I'm afraid you won't be able to touch your inheritance until you are twenty-one."

Now, I'm even more confused. "What? Why would Dad make a stipulation like that?"

Ernest adjusts his glasses and shrugs. "Such stipulations are usually made when the heir is very young and is prone to making...er...bad decisions, or is too naïve and is in danger of being cheated by the people around that person."

"I'm twenty, but I don't make stupid decision and I certainly don't hang around iffy people. My father knew that."

Ernest shrugs.

I collapse into the black giant leather chair nearest to me. I know these chairs are meant to make his clients feel comfortable, but to me it feels like something out of an Edgar Allan Poe poem. A tragedy, of course.

Never, ever did I imagine the reading of my father's will would bring me to this. I have to sit back and watch the home that has been in my mother's family for six hundred years being sold to complete strangers. They could tear those old walls down. They could change it. They could dig up my mother's grave. There is no way I can allow that.

Lori reaches over and pats my hand.

I lift my head. "There must be another way. I can't give Wotton Hall up. I promised my mother I would take care of it. That I would never let it go out of our family."

Ernest looks at me from over the rims of his glasses for a moment with a strange glint in his eyes.

"There is a way, isn't there?" I pounce immediately.

He pushes his glasses up along his nose.

I lean forward in my chair.

Lori scoots to the edge of her seat too.

"Yes, there is, but you won't like it," he says, shuffling the papers on his desk.

"What is it?"

He coughs discreetly. "Well, did you notice how you and your sister only hold forty-nine percent of the shares of your father's company?"

I shake my head.

Lori shakes hers too.

Truth is, I'd heard nothing once I knew neither my sister nor I would be inheriting Wotton Hall. "No, but carry on."

"That's because Zachary Winston Black owns the other fifty-one percent."

Lori stares at me with her mouth slack.

Zachary Winston Black! Into the fog of my confusion and despair comes the image of Zachary Black. Raven black hair, tanned; piercing, icy-gray eyes, tall, broad shouldered, a V shaped torso, sensual mouth, but my father told me one shouldn't be fooled by his gorgeous exterior. He was a very dangerous American predator. His business was asset stripping. His job was to identify businesses that appeared vulnerable and make an aggressive takeover bid on them.

"Zachary Black owns fifty-one percent of our company?" I echo in shock.

"That cannot be true!" Lori exclaims.

Ernest nods. "Yes, he bought the shares from your father about two years ago."

I shook my head to clear it. Two years ago? How come I knew nothing about any of this? My father always made a point of updating me on the happenings of his company. When we were young, he made business cards for both Lori and me to get us interested in the company.

But even more than that... how very strange to have sold shares to this particular man. Why would my father sell the controlling interest of his company, the company he had worked all his life to build, to an asset stripper he considered a very dangerous predator? The only thing I could think of was my father's business was in trouble and Zachary had swooped in.

"What does this mean? Was the business in trouble?" I ask.

"It has never been in trouble before," Lori adds.

"Oh, no. The business was fine. In fact, since Zachary came into the picture, it's never been in better shape. Selling the controlling interest to Zachary was the best thing that your father did.

My head starts to spin. "So what has he got to do with the house?"

"He doesn't, but there is a clause in the will that if anyone jointly owns more than seventy-five percent shares of the business they can move to stop the sale of the house, grounds and woods. Of course, you and your sister will not have enough on your own, but if you were to...well...marry Zachary Black... you could stop the house from being sold until you were old enough to buy it from your inheritance."

Lori gasps as she stares at him.

I too, stare at him with open-mouthed astonishment. "You can't be serious."

"I'm afraid I am. That is the only way for you to save Wotton Hall."

CHAPTER 3

Marry Zachary Black?

I feel as if I've fallen through a black vortex into an alternative universe. This can't be happening. It has to be a nightmare. It has to be.

Lori reaches over and takes my hand, squeezing it gently. "Hey," she murmurs, drawing my attention. "It's going to be okay."

I turn to face her, my mind blank with shock. I stare at her dumbfounded. She's my baby sister, only sixteen. I'm meant to be the one in charge here. It's been that way since we lost our mother, but I'm such a toxic mess she's taken charge. I have no idea what I'm meant to do anymore.

Lori tucks a loose strand of her long, dark hair behind her ear, and smiles sweetly at me. She got that sweet smile from our mother, along with her blue eyes, whereas I inherited my father's blonde-hair-brown-eyes combination. Looking at us, you would never guess we were sisters, but we are bonded by blood. I would give anything to protect her.

"It's going to be okay," she repeats. "We'll work it out somehow."

"How?"

"Maybe I can marry Zachary," she says, dimpling prettily at me.

I crack a watery smile for her benefit. "Very funny."

"Actually, I totally wouldn't mind it."

Something in her eyes makes me frown. "Don't be so silly, Lori. You're sixteen. I'm not going to let you marry a thirty-one-year old man."

She pouts. "You're such a spoil-sport."

I close my eyes. I don't need this.

"I wish Dad had never married her," Lori snarls.

There's such hatred in her voice that my eyes snap open. I didn't know she hated Victoria so much. Most of the time she was away at school and she hardly spent any time with our step mom. Only one summer vacation and Victoria was on her best behavior then, since we were staying at the home of an Italian Count and his glamorous wife.

Lori's eyes fill with tears.

"Don't cry, Lori. She made Dad happy," I lie softly. I've never blamed Dad for getting remarried. I know it's what Mom would have wanted for him, to move on and find someone who made him happy. I suppose Victoria must have made him happy, in one way or another, at least at the beginning, though I'd be damned if I could figure it out. She was a full twenty-five years younger than he was, and it was really strange that a cunning old fox like my father couldn't see through the thin veneer of what she was really after.

I guess he had been as lonely as we were when Mom passed away. Maybe he was just looking to reclaim some of that incredible connection he had with Mom, or maybe he was just looking for someone to come home to at night after a long day at the office.

Whatever it was, it didn't work out. It only took a few months for Victoria to show her true colors. To keep the fights down, she stayed up in London most of the time, only coming down twice a week. It was clear he was horribly lonely, but there wasn't a thing I could do about it.

There is something I can do now, for my family though. I stand and turn to face Ernest. "I'll call you sometime this week. Thank you for everything you've done for my family." Then I hold my hand out to my sister. "Come on, Lori. We got plans to make."

CHAPTER 4

SCARLETT

"I presume you are not here to apologize for striking me," Victoria says as soon as I am shown into the living room of her plush London apartment. She's wearing a white pantsuit and her dog is curled up on a velvet cushion next to her.

"Yes, I'm very sorry for that. I've never hit anyone in my life before. I was in shock and I wasn't thinking clearly."

"But you did find great satisfaction in it, didn't you?" she asks, a strange speculative expression in her eyes.

"No, of course not. Like I said, I wasn't thinking."

"Well, I don't accept your apology for two reasons. One, you're not really sorry and two… sorry is just a word. So if you are truly sorry, you would allow me to slap you back."

My eyes widen in astonishment. This woman is something else. I'd slapped her in a moment when I was distressed and shocked. Led by a mad instinct to stop her from uttering another insult at my dead father, I did in fact slap her, then now she just wants to slap me in the cold light of day to take revenge. Every cell in my body wants me to turn around and walk back out of her door, but the thought of asking Zachary Black to marry me is far worse than enduring a slap from Victoria. I swallow hard. "All right. You can slap me back."

As if her dog understands her animosity, it bares its teeth at me.

"It's okay, sweetie," she coos to her pet. She gets to her feet and drawing herself up to her full height; it's not that impressive, but given the spiky four-inch heels she's wearing, she towers over me.

I watch her walk towards me, her movements sure, her eyes glittering with unholy excitement at the thought of taking revenge, of hurting me.

She stops two feet in front of me and smiles, a smug horrible smile. "Ready?"

"Yes."

Her hand swings back and flies in an arc towards my face. The sound of her hand connecting with my cheek startles me. My head snaps to the side, but I jerk it back in her direction instantly. My cheek burns like it is on fire, but I do not touch it. "Are we even now?" I ask, even as my eyes sting with tears that I blink back.

She will not have the satisfaction of seeing me cry.

"Yes," she breathes the answer out heavily.

I lift my chin and we stare at each other.

She smiles slowly. "I've been wanting to do that for a very, very long time." Then she walks away from me. Sitting down next to her dog again, she massages the palm she used to slap me with. "So what are you here for?" As if she didn't know.

"I came here to ask you to sell the house to me and Lori."

She puts on a totally fake expression of confusion. Like a cat playing with a mouse, she plans to draw out my humiliation. "But I was given to understand you won't be able to touch your inheritance until you are twenty-one. What were you planning to buy the house with? Tears?"

"We'll...Lori and I will hand over the stocks for the business. I've spoken to the accountant; it is worth twice what the house is."

"I don't think so," she replies coolly, stroking her little dog.

I have to fight the urge to push her right off her chair. She looks so smug. She doesn't even want that house, but she is enjoying the leverage it gives her over the two of us. Did Dad really think that she would be better for Wotton Hall than either of his daughters? I wish I could speak to him one last time. Ask him what the hell he had been thinking, making sure that none of us got anything we wanted? We only buried my father a few days before, and I am already feeling angry at him. And guilty, for feeling angry at him.

"Victoria, please, I'm begging you," I continue, trying to keep my voice steady and knowing that I'm doing a bad job at it. "Just think of what you are saying. The stocks are worth almost double what the house is worth. Please. This house belonged to my mother's family. My father had no right to give it to you. He was only holding it for me. Please. You don't want it. Just sell it to us."

"Who'd have thought? I never thought I'd see the day! The high and mighty Princess groveling at my feet."

"Yes, I am begging. Please don't let that house go to anyone else. Do it for my father's sake."

"I guess I could do it for Simon's sake." She sighs. "But I really don't want to wait until you are twenty-one to collect my inheritance."

There is something sly in her eyes, but I ignore it and clutch at the hope I see her holding out. "Look, I think I could use my stocks as collateral and borrow the money from one of Mom's old friends. I know she would give it to me."

She looks at me curiously. "Someone would lend you that much money?"

"Yes, yes, I could get the money for you. Just think, you wouldn't have to pay any Estate Agent's fee or have to put up with any kind of delay. I can arrange for you to have the money straight-away."

She looks at me as if she is seriously considering the idea. "Really?"

"Yes, I could," I cry eagerly.

"Hmmm…it is an idea, but before I commit to it, can you tell me what MA stands for?"

All my enthusiasm comes crashing to a halt. "What?"

"MA," she repeats politely. "You know, you and your sister used to refer to me as MA. I just want to know what it stands for."

I clear my throat. "It's just a little thing between us. We…

umm…like to give everyone little pet names. It doesn't mean anything. It's just for fun."

She smiles. It's a good smile. It's the one she wore on her wedding day to my father. If you didn't know better, you could never tell it was completely fake. "So what does it stand for then, this fun name your sister and you have given me?"

It is at that moment that I think I recognize I have been taken down the garden path. Even if I had the money in cash right then and there, she would not have allowed us to buy Mom's house, just out of pure spite. But that determined part of me couldn't stop. Even if there was a one percent chance she could be persuaded to sell Mom's house to me I had to stay and try for it. "MA stands for Marie Antoinette."

"Marie Antoinette?" She frowns. "The name is familiar, but I can't put my finger it on it. Remind me."

"She was the last Queen of France," I say quietly.

The frown clears. "Wasn't she the one who was beheaded?"

"Yes, but we only called you that because you like luxury." I sweep my hand around at the lavish gold and gilt furnishing she has surrounded herself with.

"You think I'm so stupid, don't you? You and that brat thinking you are better than me. Well, looks like the roles have reversed, eh? I'm the one with the big prize and you're the one with nothing."

"You're a smart woman, Victoria. Why would you cut your nose off to spite your face? Selling to me would mean you would get double the value of the house." I hate that note of desperation that has crept into my voice.

She smiles sweetly at me. "Like you said, I'm a smart woman. I didn't sit on my hands waiting for your father to kick the bucket. I went out and found me another man to take care of me. So I'm not desperate for cash. In fact, I'd rather burn that godforsaken house to the ground than let you have it."

I realize almost too late that there is no point hanging around a second longer. She isn't going to let me have the house. She hates me that much. I turn on my heel and march to the door, but I'm not beat yet. I still have one nuclear option left.

CHAPTER 5

SCARLETT

A nd that's how I find myself an hour later walking up to Zachary Black's secretary, while trying to gather up the courage to ask to see him without an appointment. She is already eyeing me even from afar with impatience and contempt. She's probably wondering what business someone like me has with the great Zachary. Or maybe she thinks I'm one of his more hopeless hook-ups, back around because I don't know how to take no for an answer.

If only she knew.

A name tag announces her as Dahlia Dewbury. "Can I help you?" she asks as I approach her desk, but her frosty voice makes it clear that she believes there is absolutely nothing she can do for me other than send me away.

"Hello," I greet, stretching my mouth into a friendly smile. "My name is Scarlett Johnson and I'd like to see Mr. Black. I won't take long I just need to talk to him about some of the holdings he has in my father's company, Johnson Sparrow."

Those words and the name of my father's company had been

enough for the receptionist on the ground floor to instantly give me access to the elevators, but Dahlia turns out to be a harder nut to crack. Her expression remains unchanged and unimpressed. "Do you have an appointment with him?" she asks.

I shake my head. "No, but this is *very* important."

"I'm sure it is, but he's in a meeting right now."

"Tell him that it's Scarlett Johnson. Tell him I need to speak to him about my father's business."

"Like I said he's in a meeting," she tells me firmly, "but if you want to leave a name and number, I'll see if I can set up something tomorrow or—"

"No," I interrupt, putting my palms on her desk and leaning forward. "I can't wait until tomorrow. I need to see him now." I feel guilty for acting like a spoilt brat, but I honestly don't believe her that he cannot be interrupted, and I know if I walk out of here, I'm not going to have the nerve to follow up on this. If not for the adrenaline still rushing through my veins from my meeting with Victoria, I might never even have plucked up the courage to do this. Something about Zachary Black makes the hairs at the back of my neck stand and confuses me.

"For the last time," she said, her voice cold and unyielding, "Mr. Black is in a meeting and after that he is straight onto another one so there is zero chance you will be able to see him today.

"I need to see him," I cry in desperation. There is so much at stake for me. "You don't understand. This is important. This is so important—"

"Yes, I'm sure it is a matter of life and death, but he's in a meeting and can't be disturbed." There is undisguised sarcasm in her voice. She gets to her feet. "So I'm going to have to ask you to leave, Miss. Johnson. Otherwise, I'll have no option but call security to escort you out."

Before she can say another word, I straighten and run past her and down the corridor towards a large executive looking door that has to be his office. I know that I am acting crazy. That I could land myself in a whole heap of trouble for this, but I can't walk away now. He's right through that door, and I'm not going to leave here without speaking to him.

"Hey! Excuse me! Excuse me!" Dahlia calls after me, but I ignore her and keep heading for the large door. I decide that I've already forgone the formality of knocking. Taking a deep breath, I just open and push the heavy door in.

And there he is... dressed in an impeccable suit. Looking like a billion dollars.

His dark head swivels around at first in irritation, then his eyebrow cocks up in astonishment. The man opposite him seems confused by my interruption, but I stand my ground.

"I need to speak to you," I say quickly. "Urgently."

For a couple of seconds, he does nothing, just stares at me as if I had two horns on my head, then he turns to the man. "Could you give us a minute, Harvey?"

Immediately, the man gets to his feet and starts heading towards the door. I move to let him pass, his eyes are on me and full of avid curiosity. Exhaling the breath I'd been holding, I level my gaze at Zachary Black, and feel the thing that happens every time I've met him at the industry parties my father used to take me to: little feather-light tendrils of desire snaking across my skin, making me shiver. I try to ignore the confusing reaction my body has to him. Why he makes me feel that way is a mystery. I hate men like him. It is galling, especially since I know he has no such reaction to me. He's always got a different woman on his arm, and he always looks at me like a little girl who should be sitting at the kids' table.

I watch his eyes run down my body. Then he stands and starts walking towards me. As he gets closer, my stomach tightens crazily. His aftershave hits my nostrils and I think I am going to faint.

I must be stone-cold crazy to do this, he is almost certainly going to refuse me. He's probably going to laugh in my face and tell me to try someone who is actually interested, but I have to try. He is my last hope of keeping Wotton Hall. I will never forgive myself if I don't at least give it a try. It might seem crazy – it might *be* crazy – but I have to try.

CHAPTER 6

ZACH

"**Y**ou care to tell me what you're doing barging in on my meeting with no explanation?" I ask, pushing the door shut behind Harvey, my agent for Asia. We had just barely finished our meeting when she shows up. He flew in last night for the express purpose of meeting me today and updating me on an issue so sensitive, it could not be discussed on any electronic communication. He also has a flight out in five hours, so I should have just booted her out and told her to come back later, but...

This is Scarlett Johnson.

She'd just turned eighteen when I first met her. I'd been invited to a huge company affair her father threw, and it was the first one she'd been allowed to attend. She was all wide-eyed and as wobbly as a day-old antelope in her tall heels. When her small soft hand slipped into mine, I felt like I'd been kicked in the gut. I tried to hide it, but her father was a wily old fox. He escorted her off before we could get beyond hello. Not that I blamed him. With the kind of reputation I had with women, I'd have done the same if she were my daughter.

Women don't tend to stick in my head too well. That's what happens when you've been through so many of them, I guess. Nobody stands out when you're going through them as random hook-ups that could fit into my tight schedule. But for some inexplicable reason, Scarlett remains unforgettable. Sometimes I still remember her hand in mine. Her eyes so enormous and innocent I wanted to punch out the lights of any man who looked at her.

After that time, I stayed well clear of her whenever we ended up at the same social events. It's for the best. I knew she is the kind of girl who spells trouble. Big trouble. And quite simply, I didn't trust myself around her. Around her, I became a primitive stranger who wanted to throw her over my shoulders, and take her straight to my bedroom, then throw away the key.

Staying clear didn't solve the problem though. Every time I saw her, I swear she got that bit more delectable. Those curves, the mile-long legs, the shining long, blonde hair, and those chocolate brown eyes that told a different story than the rest of her face.

I lean against the door and look at her. Since our first meeting, this is the closest I've been to her. Her left cheek is red and swollen and her blonde hair is pulled back into a ponytail, as it swings angrily with every gesture she makes. The last thing I expected is to find her standing in my office glaring up at me like I'd done something wrong.

"You want to sit down?" I ask, pointing at the chair Harvey had just vacated.

She huffs to herself, and then does as she's told.

I start to walk towards my chair.

The door behind me opens, and Dahlia sticks her head around it. She glares at Scarlett then turns her attention to me.

"Security has been called, Sir," she tells me.

I shake my head and wave my hand. "Tell them that they're not going to be needed."

She frowns. "Are you sure?"

"Yes, I'm sure."

She lingers for a moment longer in the doorway before she ducks away again, pulling the door shut behind her.

I sit down and turn my attention back to the woman before me. She looks exhausted, as though she hasn't slept properly in days. It has only been a few days since her father passed. She's probably still dealing with everything that comes with that.

With Dahlia gone, Scarlett turns her attention back to me. Her eyes are wide. "I just found out that you have a stake in my father's company," she explains quickly. "And I need to use it for something."

"Okay, hold up." I lift my hand to stop her in her tracks. "You just found out about this? Your father didn't tell you about it?"

She shakes her head. "No, and that's the weird part, because he let me and my sister in on the business so much, my sister banned him from talking business to her when she was seven years old."

"Right," I say softy.

"Anyway, during the reading of the will, our family solicitor told me that you have a stake in the house and surrounding land and woods as part of your deal. Is that right? Does that still stand?"

I fall silent for a moment. I hadn't so much as thought about what I owned in Simon's company for years. It was so long ago that I bailed him out and since then, he had compensated me for it handsomely I've never thought much about the deal other than the yearly profit my accountants file away. I had no interest in anything like that, but if she were talking wills and solicitors, it would seem my shares have picked up some power.

"Yes, I believe it is something like that. I never looked very deeply into it, but it is not a straightforward ownership. For some reason, your father insisted on writing it into the deal as some kind security, but it isn't as if I could sell it if I wanted to."

She nods quickly, distractedly, which tells me she needs me for something.

"What's going on?" I ask.

She stands and begins to pace. "My father left the house and the land to our stepmother." She spits the words out like she can't bear saying them. "And she wants to sell it, but not to us.

I stare at her astonished. Why on earth would Simon do that? I've met her stepmother and she doesn't even pretend she's not an out and out gold digger. In fact, the last time I met him, he hinted at his regrets in marrying her.

"So," Scarlett continues, "my sister and I will lose our inheritance unless...well, unless I can get the rights to that deal that you made with my father."

I lean back against the chair. "What are you offering in exchange for that?"

"My sister and I are willing to give you our shares in the company," she replies. "All of them. It's forty-nine percent and it would give you complete control over the company."

Damn. Okay, now this did seem like a pretty tempting deal. That company is old-school, but it would look good on my roster if I could get it there. I don't betray any emotions. My eyes keep straying to her cheek. I can already guess where she got that injury from. "And what do I need to do for that?" I ask. "Sign over the rights to the deal to you? I'm not sure exactly how it would work. I'd have to get my solicitor to—"

"You would need to marry me."

CHAPTER 7

ZACH

My jaw drops. There's no way I heard her correctly. Because never, in a million years, would this woman walk in here and look me in the eyes and act like what she just said could be even remotely close to logical. "Can you repeat that? I don't think I heard you correctly."

"Look, I don't want this any more than you do," she says, grimacing slightly. "It'll just be a marriage in name only."

I should be insulted but I'm not. There are too many women in this city who wouldn't exactly be grimacing at the thought of me as their husband. But that isn't what I am, and I'm not sure it's who I'll ever be. Still, the thought of getting to play house with a woman who looked like this...my eyes trail down her body, the slim legs exposed beneath her skirt. Yeah, I could live with it.

"The only way to stop my stepmother from selling the house is if we team up and become the majority shareholder and veto her sale. My sister and I don't have enough shares, but we will if we team up with you. However, your shares are not transferable and cannot be bought or sold or given away," she continues. "In order for me to get the rights to it, I have to marry you."

I stare at her for a long moment. I've heard plenty of crazy business pitches in my time, but this has to be one of the wildest. The way she's looking at me, I can tell that she's willing to do anything to get what she wants from me. And man, there is some part of me that's tempted to exploit that. I would love to just lean across the desk right now and slip my hands between her milky thighs, cup that soft...

"Will you do it?" she asks, cutting off my lustful train of thought.

Maybe if she hadn't cut off that train of thought. I shake my head. "The house is not worth as much as the shares."

"I don't care," she says. "That house has been in my mother's family for six hundred years. I must have it."

"I can't," I replied. "I'm sorry. It's not—"

"You have to listen to me!" she pleads. "This is the only chance I have of keeping my home. You understand that, right? You see how important this is to me?"

"Look, I have no doubt that you'll find another way to keep hold of your house," I tell her. "This isn't—"

"I'll do anything you want me to," she says suddenly. Her eyes are pinned to mine.

Suddenly, I feel something wild and fiery run through my system. God, I want her. Maybe it's all the time I've spent thinking she's off limits. That I could never have her, but the thought of her doing anything, *anything* at all to please me gives me an instant hard-on. My dick starts to beg for her.

Meeting her gaze steadily, I get to my feet. This is a deal with plenty in it for me, so it's not the wildest thought in the world for me to go through with it, but I'd be lying if I said this had anything at all to do with my business acumen anymore.

As I get closer, I can see the outline of her breasts through the thin fabric of her shirt. She must be wearing one of those lacy bras because her nipples are pressing against the fabric. I can almost feel them between my lips, taste the bright cherry freshness under my tongue...

"Anything?" I ask softly as I reach out and touch her cheek. I can almost feel the heat burning off

her.

She catches her breath and drops her gaze. She knows exactly what I'm saying to her, even if she tries to play dumb. A woman like her should be fucked every day.

"Anything," she agrees at last, her voice low as she turns those deep brown eyes back up to me.

They are flecked with speckles of gold, something I hadn't noticed until now.

She moves an inch closer to me, and her chest is rising and falling swiftly. Her breath is a little ragged.

I take a step away from her, walk back to my seat, thenlean back and look up at her. Her skirt has ridden up by an inch or two, and I wonder, idly, if she is wearing any panties under there or if she prefers to go bare. I bet the flavor of her would bring a man to his knees. "Pull your skirt up and show me your pussy," I surprise myself by saying.

Her eyes become as wide as saucers. "What? Now? Here?" she splutters, almost incoherent with shock.

I shrug. "You said… anything."

She bites her plump bottom lip and looks like a scared rabbit. "What if someone comes in?"

I smile. "No one will."

"Does this mean you'll marry me?"

"Sure," I drawl. When I came to work this morning it never crossed my mind, my day would turn out like this.

She grabs the material of her skirt around her thighs, then pauses.

I see her face turn red. Aww… sweet. She is shy. I raise an eyebrow.

Then with an icy glare at me, she pulls the material up to her hips. Her panties are white silk with white lace. All very pure and virginal.

I hear my own breath come out of me hard.

Then she dips her fingers into the waistband and quickly pulls her panties down her legs.

My eyes are riveted at her bare pussy.

Oh, fuck!

She is clean shaven.

My mouth waters and my cock is so hard it fucking hurts. I

have to fight not to go up to her and bury my head between those sweet thighs. In my head, I can already hear her screaming my name. It is while she is pulling her panties up again when I notice the wet spot on them. Heck, she is as turned on as I am.

"I'll draw up a pre-nuptial agreement as soon as I get the chance." My voice sounds hoarse and thick. I know what is running through her mind. I have been with enough women to know when they want me, and this one wants me. I can tell that she's not going to have any problem carrying out her wifely duties when the time comes. Her father has kept her locked away from men like me her entire life and yet... he has driven her right into my arms.

"And you can take a look over it and make sure everything is to your liking," I continue.

She smooths her hands over her skirt. Her cheeks are red.

I can tell that I have shaken her and I am glad to see it. "You can move in with me at once," I order.

Her eyes widen. "What?"

"Surely, you don't want to give your stepmother cause to question the validity of our marriage," I explain. "She and her lawyers are going to be looking at this very hard, Scarlett..."

She nods, still avoiding my eyes. "Yes, I suppose so..."

"Besides, you will have to live to your side of the bargain," I remind, raising my eyebrows at her pointedly.

She flushes bright red.

Damn, she looks so cute when she does that. It's hard to keep from reaching over and kissing that ripe mouth, feeling its softness against mine. I wonder if she's had much experience, or if she's still fresh to this game. She certainly doesn't have a boyfriend, because there's no way in hell any guy in his right mind would allow a woman like that out of his sight for an instant.

Especially, not around someone like me.

"Of course," she agrees breathlessly.

I lean back in my seat and grin. In terms of a business meeting, this has to be one of the most successful. Absolutely, one of the best deals that I look forward to putting to bed. Literally.

CHAPTER 8

SCARLETT

I arrive outside his house and gaze up at the place that's going to be my home for the next...well, I don't know how long. I guess, until the house issue is sorted out. I feel a twist of excitement and dread wash around my system. Because I don't know if I'm going to be able to keep whatever I felt back there when it had just been the two of us in the office under wraps for too long.

Everything happened so fast I'd hardly had time to keep on top of it. I had turned up at his office, and within a few minutes, he'd agreed to take my shares of the company off my hands if he would help me make the claim on the house and the land. Which was what I wanted, of course, but then...

I can't shake the memory of what I did. Pulling down my panties and showing my bits like that. I've never done that in my life and yet—it hadn't disgusted, or shocked me. No, it had turned me on.

And the way he looked at me. God, the *hunger* in his eyes. Sure, other men have looked at me with desire, even lust, but nobody, and I mean, nobody has ever looked at me the way he did. Like he was starving. Like he could hardly hold himself back from streaking across the room and taking me right there and then on his office floor.

Funny thing is… I wanted him to do it. I really did. And it wasn't because I wanted the house either. If he'd asked me to get down on my knees and take his cock in my mouth, I would have done it. I wanted him and I knew he wanted me too.

But what he doesn't know is…that…well, I'm a virgin.

Yeah, shocking at my age, but I've never had sex. In fact, I've never gone past second base in my life. I've never even really had a boyfriend. I was focused on my studies when I was in school, then after Mom became sick I decided not to leave her side. Even though I had my heart set on becoming a fashion designer, the little time she had left was too precious to waste going to class.

Not even Dad ranting and raving could change my mind so he pulled strings at the London School of Fashion and got permission for me receive recorded lessons. Long story short, I got left on the shelf.

Poor Zachary. What a nasty surprise he's going to get when he gets me into his bed and realizes I don't have a clue how to satisfy a man.

With that in mind, I made sure to read through the pre-nup carefully, making sure there is nothing there that is going to catch me out down the line, especially if he becomes dissatisfied with my performance. I showed Ernest the document too and he said it all seemed pretty standard. An agreement that we are going to stay together for as long as it takes for me to get the house and the land and for him to get the stocks transferred over to him. No more, no less.

Which is just fine by me. I'm just unbelievably grateful he agreed to help me at all. Especially, considering how being married might affect his ability to pull in women. I've never seen him with the same woman twice. Each one more beautiful than the one before. A worm of worry digs into my brain that I will not compare to them, but I push the thoughts aside impatiently.

It's not a relationship, Scarlett. It's a mutually advantageous arrangement.

In fact, I have no idea if he's planning to keep up his usual affairs while we're married. I suppose he will. There is nothing in the contract to stop him. Something feels off, but I tell myself it doesn't matter either way, as long as he is discreet. I just need to borrow his name on paper so I can keep Victoria from selling the house long enough for her to realize that...she either sells to me or she sells to no one.

"Miss Johnson?"

A voice draws my attention as I climb out of the cab. I look up to an impeccably-dressed older man with the ghost of a smile on his face.

"Yes, that's me," I say, clutching my overnight bag close to my body.

"I'm Arnold," he introduces himself. "I help keep things running smoothly around here. May I take your bag and show you to your room?"

"The bag isn't heavy so I'm all right," I say with a smile, thinking of all the bags my sister had when I helped her move into the London apartment Dad left for both of us. "But yes, please show me to my room."

I follow him up the stone steps to the house. Wotton Hall is an impressive old house, but nothing compared to Avebury Court. It's the kind of place that wouldn't look amiss in a fairytale movie. Thick stone walls, sixteen-foot tall ceilings, tall windows, Greek and Roman themed friezes on the walls, ashen pink, tans, pale blues and white detailing. There's also antique furniture everywhere I turn. Massive gilded paintings adorn the walls, and modern sculptures are scattered through the reception area.

It is an awe-inspiring house with the kind of decadence that my best friend, Molly would have rolled her eyes at. I should bring her here sometime. She'll find the whole thing pretty funny.

CHAPTER 9

SCARLETT

"There you are," Zach announces, coming down the stairs and catching me off-guard. "Arnold, could you take her bag to her room?"

"Of course, sir," he replies. He takes my bag from me and heads for the stairs.

This is the first time I've seen Zach out of a suit. He's wearing a pair of black jeans and a pale blue tee. It makes his grey eyes even more piercing than normal and it increases that animal grace about him.

"Hi," I greet softly. I pull out a smile for him, even though I feel like I am about to keel over with nervousness.

"Good to see you," Zach drawls.

I can swear there is a hint of real warmth to his voice. But I must be imagining that. It's hardly on-brand for him to be anything but the cold ruthless businessman. Though, maybe there's more to him in his off-hours than I've given him credit for.

"You too," I reply as he arrives in front of me.

He smiles slowly and sexily at me.

Butterflies start flapping around inside my belly. It's so very strange to think I'm going to be married to this man; the wedding is planned for as soon as his team of people can manage it. This isn't at all how I imagined I would be getting married for the first time, but desperate times, desperate measures, and all that.

"Let me show you around," he says suavely, and he reaches for my hand casually.

I feel a jolt of electricity run up from my fingers where they connect with his. He must know what he's doing to me. When he touched my cheek in his office, I felt as though I was going to combust on the spot. All this time, I thought he just saw me as an irritating little girl, but the way he was looking at me then told me I'd been wrong. Dead wrong. About as wrong as it was possible to be.

"So, this is where I'm going to be living, huh?" I croak.

He grins at me and nods. "Can't think you'll have much reason to venture out. I have everything you could possibly want in here."

"Oh, yeah?" I reply, cocking an eyebrow. "Like what?"

"I spend a lot of time in here," he replies, as he pushes open a door that leads us straight into an enormous pool room.

"No way." I laugh, incredulous and slightly relieved that he let go of my hand. It was hard to think when our skin is touching. I look around me curiously. I've only seen things like this in music videos. Yeah, I come from a family with money, but we are old money. We don't spend it on putting in outrageous stuff like full-size pools and marble Corinthian columns everywhere you look.

"Too much?" he asks.

I shrug. "Not if you're living inside a rapper's music video."

He throws his head back and laughs. The sound echoes in the hot, damp air.

I watch the muscles in his strong, tanned throat work with fascination. God, this man is so beautiful.

When he stops laughing, he looks down at me, his eyes twinkling still with amusement. "I agree with you, but I inherited all this, and never took the time to change anything. To be honest I'm usually so involved in my work I hardly even notice my surroundings."

I frown at the confession. Suddenly, he seems too human and that is not a good thing. I don't want to start liking him. "I guess it does the job," I mutter, my gaze sliding away from his.

"There's a gym on the other side. I have a personal trainer who comes by a few times a week, if you feel like checking it out."

"I'm not really a gym bunny," I admit, eyeing the pool with interest, then I turn away. I should have brought a bikini or something. Silly of me, but I didn't imagine I would be moving into any place as absurdly luxurious as this.

"Well, plenty of time to become one," he replies evenly. He pulls the door shut and heads off down the corridor next to it.

He doesn't take my hand again, and I can't help but feel a little pouty over it, which I know is crazy.

"The library is just down here," he explains, as he opens another door.

I smile when I see the enormous room filled with enough books to fuel a whole college class for at least a couple of semesters. I used to love reading, but since Mom passed, I haven't made as much time for it as I would have liked. Maybe now that I'm here I can get back into it again. It's not like there's going to be a lot for me to stress out about, with the butler and everything.

"Do you like to read?" I ask, stepping inside and brushing past him on the way. He smells so good, like clean skin, sandalwood and something mysterious.

"Well, I didn't just have this put in for show," he mocks.

I quickly move away from his tantalizing scent and trail my fingers over the first shelf, the one nearest the door. In the middle of the room, there are a couple of massive armchairs that I can already imagine myself settling into with a good book. In fact, it sounds just heavenly. "Oh hey, I love this one!" I exclaim as I pluck a book from the shelves. *Spectacles By Night*, by Anton Raider. The copy is even the same one I had when I was growing up.

"Really?" he asks, sounding surprised.

I nod. "I read it for the first time when I was fifteen or so. It was the first adult book I was allowed to read, and I just thought it was the greatest thing ever." I glance up then, and notice he is giving me a funny look. "What?" I ask, nonplussed. "What is it?"

"*Spectacles By Night* is one of my favorites, too," he replies, taking the book from me and thumbing through the pages, almost fondly. "I've never actually met anyone else who's read it." He looks up and our gazes collide.

I feel heat rush into my cheeks. "That's because you've been hanging around with the wrong kind of people," I joke lamely, and I earn a smile from him. I like it when he smiles at me. It sets off something deep down in my belly, something that makes me feel warm and fuzzy. And a little off-balance at the same time, but in a good way.

"Maybe I have," he murmurs, as he slides the book back on to the shelf beside me. His eyes flick down to my mouth.

I can tell he's thinking the same thing I am. I swallow hard and tear my gaze away from his. He is standing so close to me, I could just turn my head and kiss him if I wanted to...not that I want to. Or, more importantly, not that I'm going to let myself. I would have to be crazy to let myself fall for a man like him, for a man with his reputation. Even letting myself flirt a little is dangerous. I've had quite enough excitement in my life for the time being as it is. I need to set some rules for our relationship or I will end up making a fool of myself.

"I just want to make one thing clear," I tell him firmly, or as firmly as I can since my voice is shaking. An unreasonable, illogical part of me wants to go through with this, wants him to lean forward and kiss me, push me up against these books, pull my body close.

But I won't.

I have more important things to focus on right now. I have a promise to keep to my mother, and a home to secure for my sister. I'm not going to let some fleeting attraction to someone I know I don't even like, get in the way of that.

"Go ahead," he urges, but already I can hear the coolness that has come into his voice.

"I'm not here because I like you and other than the physical aspect of our bargain, nothing can happen between us," I say. "I know how you run your business, and it's not something I want to get involved with, not beyond this...this fake marriage. The way you just pick over dying companies...yeah, it's really not something I can get behind."

"I get it," he replies, his face impassive, not showing a hint of emotion. If he is pissed at me, he's not letting me know about it.

I should have stopped there, but I couldn't. I hear more words coming out of my mouth, "I might like the same books as you, but I'm not like you," I continue, running my fingers through my hair. "Is that clear?"

He levels his gaze with mine, and a smile curls up along his lips.

This smile makes my belly ache for something I know I've never wanted before.

"Crystal," he says softly.

CHAPTER 10

ZACH

She crosses her arms over her chest as though she is trying to cut me off from her body. A moment ago, it felt as though we'd been on the brink of something real, but I'm starting to wonder if I'd invented that fantasy in my head.

I am irritated and I refuse to show it. I know I shouldn't let her get to me, but there's something about her that has already begun to worm its way beneath my skin. Maybe it's just that I wasn't allowed to go near her for so long and now, there is nothing standing in the way. Well, nothing but her high and mighty declarations that she wants nothing to do with lowly me, of course.

"Don't worry," I say as nonchalantly as I can. "You'll only need to perform your wifely duties until I get bored of you." I see a flicker of hurt pass over her face, and I ignore it. I'm not here to soothe her ego. I'm here for business and to have her like I've always wanted to.

"And I'm sure that won't take too long," she mutters.

"Probably not."

Her mouth parts with a small gasp.

Now, I know I've really hurt her. "Come on, let me show you where you're staying," I throw over my shoulder as I turn away from her.

She follows me out of the library silently.

The muscles in my shoulders feel tense and strained. We jumped so damn fast from actually getting along with one another to this prickly atmosphere that it's giving me whiplash. I didn't like not being the one in control... it didn't suit me at all. I didn't get where I have in the business world because I let other people tell me how to play the game, that is for damn sure...

No point me getting all twisted up about her. I'll get her out of my system then go back to the life I am used to. Women on tap and no strings. I have an apartment in the city that I normally use for hook-ups, making sure none of them actually get to come to this place. This is my hideaway, and it's being invaded even as we speak by a woman who has just shown open contempt for me.

I lead her up the stairs to the bedroom.

Scarlett follows close behind, her arms still crossed over her chest in an attitude of rejection.

Her perfume is sweet with undertones of something spicy. It hides her real scent and I hate that. "This is where you'll be staying," I tell her, pushing the door to the bedroom open.

She steps inside and after a quick glance, she turns to me with her eyebrows raised. "This is your bedroom."

"Yeah, I'm aware of that," I answer dryly.

She laughs, but there isn't much mirth in it. "You really think I'm just going to move into your bedroom?"

I cross my arms over my chest. "Look at it this way. The sooner you bore me the sooner you'll get your own room."

"Fine," she snaps.

"You want a hand unpacking your things?"

She shakes her head. "I can handle that on my own," she shoots back. She goes to pick up one of her bags, but it slips out of her hand, and lands with a thud on the floor.

"What have you got in there, bricks?" I ask as I lean down to grab it for her. When I straighten, we're standing so close I can see her teeth buried in her freshly licked bottom lip and her eyes glowing with that rare gold tinge that makes my gut burn for her.

"Zach," she murmurs, her pupils dilated. "I..."

Before she can say another word, I capture that plump mouth with mine.

It may look like I'm playing a risky game since she just told me she thinks I'm an asshole. That she wouldn't be sleeping with me out of choice. But guess what? I don't fucking believe her. I think she's a liar. She'd been so turned on in my office, I could fucking smell her little pussy. So, this... this is just testing the waters. If I hook nothing, fine, I'll sleep over at my apartment in the city and she can stay here and play the Ice Princess by herself.

But if I catch...

47

She lets out a moan as I part her eager lips with my tongue and taste her for the first time. Damn, she feels so good. I slide my hands down her sides and grasping her hips, slam her body into mine. I'm uncharacteristically rough, but I can't stop myself. I want to feel her body. I want to make it mine.

Fuck, I want to own her utterly.

She sinks against me and rakes her fingers through my hair, grasping, and pulling me closer to her. As if she can't get enough. She moves her hips back against my cock, her movements as sensuous as a snake. Her body wants my cock.

So here we are, in my bedroom, her tongue in my mouth and her soft, supple body against mine, and all I want to do is throw her on my bed, rip off her clothes and—

A knock at the door draws my attention, but she is so into it, she doesn't even hear it. I pull away from her and she looks up at me, her cheeks flushed, her mouth swollen, and her eyes wide and glassy. "What is it?" she whispers. The discreet knock comes again and this time she hears it and jumps back like a startled deer. She is so embarrassed she can't so much as look me in the eyes.

It's so damned cute. I can't remember the last time a woman was embarrassed because someone knocked on the door while we were making out. "Come in," I call.

The door opens. "Sorry to interrupt, Sir," Arnold says in his formal voice, but there is a flicker of amusement on his face. "But there's a phone call for you. They say it's urgent, can't wait."

I open my mouth to tell him that they're just going to have to wait, but then I glance over at Scarlett and change my mind. Her body is tightly strung, her breath is coming in short, sharp bursts, and she is looking at me with blatant desire. If I send Arnold away, I could have her right here and now. And even though I'm so turned on I'll probably have to relieve myself soon, I want to make her wait for it. The longer she waits the sweeter her release will be.

"I'll be right down," I reply. "Thanks, Arnold." I shoot a look at Scarlett.

She looks flabbergasted.

Good! Then I walk out of the room and leave her to overheat with the promise of our unfinished business.

CHAPTER 11

SCARLETT

I stand here, mouth open, staring after him. What the hell...? I am sure he was into it as much as I was, but he walks away from me like it is nothing.

Hell, I can still smell his aftershave on my skin.

I close my eyes and let his scent wash over me. It pulses through my whole body. I want him back. No... more than that.... I need him back. I need to touch him again. I want to kiss him. I've never been kissed like that before in my life and it made me feel like my whole body was being set on fire.

Why wouldn't I want more of that?

I frown thinking about him. He must have known I was desperate for it, but could he have known I've never done that before? Maybe that's why he found it so easy to walk away from me? Maybe I am a terrible kisser? The thought thrums in my head, panic, and humiliation running through me all at once.

But no. That can't be it either.

The look he gave me when he left the room promised more was coming later. Now that I think of it, the whole exercise must have been a tease. Maybe, when he is done, he will come back here and finish what he started. The thought thrills me and exciting pulses shoot down my spine, which is weird considering I just told him, a few minutes ago I didn't want to get involved with him. And I still don't. I don't want to get involved emotionally with him, but that doesn't mean I can't allow myself to have a little fun while I'm here.

I hang around for fifteen minutes before I realize he is not coming back. He just left me high and dry to pine for him. I glance to the bed. Damn him. I don't masturbate a lot. The last year has been sad. Taking care of a sick man doesn't put any sexy thoughts into your head. Also, there had been no Zack around to arouse me.

I make sure that the door is closed before I slide on top of the covers and slip my hand down my panties to find my clit. It is still swollen and throbbing.

I move my fingers against my pussy, pushing back against them, needing more pressure, more. I close my eyes and pretend they are his fingers, brushing against my clit. I imagine his hard body is here with me on the bed.

What would he do to me if he were here?

I let my imagination take control, and soon enough my head is filled with images of us in his office. This time, he doesn't let me pull my panties back on. He orders me to come sit on the desk in front of him and spread my legs wide. I obey him. His face is only a foot away from my open pussy. In his eyes, I see that insatiable hunger again. He caresses my clit, his heavy-lidded eyes on mine as he watches my reactions. I feel an explosive shudder of lust running through me making my body jump as his fingers circle my clit. Oh God, I'm going to come.

"You've never been touched by a man before, have you Scarlett?" he asks, as he plays with my pussy, his fingers tracing around the outside of my hole.

I nod. How would it feel to have him inside me there? Would it hurt? He knows what he is doing, he would know how to make it work...how to make it feel good for me, even though I've never done it before.

"Saving all this for my cock, huh?" he murmurs, plunging his thick fingers into my pussy.

I push a finger inside of myself and gasp at the wetness, the slickness, the smoothness within me. And I'm taken aback by how damn good it feels. I thought it would hurt, but instead, I find myself adding another finger, just wanting to find out what it would be like to have his cock inside me.

I know my fingers are a poor substitute for what he can give me. He could wrap his arms around me and pull me close, kiss me just like he kissed me today, his tongue deep in my mouth, exploring me like he never wanted to stop. I find myself lifting my hips and moving back against my fingers helplessly, a small moan escaping my lips. I know there are other people in this house and I could be busted in the act at any moment, but I don't give a damn. I just want to feel that release, the release I have been craving since he touched my sex with his eyes in his office and told me, without words, that he was going to make me his...

When my climax rolls through me, I have to press my lips together to keep from screaming. The pleasure bursts through me, my nerve-endings lighting up like a Christmas tree. It is so real I can almost feel the touch of his sweet mouth on mine again, even though he feels so far away.

I let myself come to stillness again, and gaze up at the ceiling.

As the fog of pleasure clears and I return to my body all over again, I wonder what the hell I am doing. I just made myself come in his bed! How could I have lost control so completely and so quickly? I haven't even been in this house a full hour yet, and he has already found a way to push me to the point where I can't take it without giving myself some relief.

Then I remember the look on his face and I realize that this is probably exactly how he wants me. He wants me desperate for him. He wants me starving for his touch. Because, I'm sure, he plans on feeding me again. And he wants to make sure I'm ravenous for him when that time comes.

I close my eyes. I am so exhausted from everything that has happened the last few days that sleep comes to me almost at once. I inhale the scent of him still left on his pillow from the night before, and let myself drift off.

CHAPTER 12

When my eyes flutter open, back to wakefulness, it is morning. I can tell from the buttery yellow light filtering through the gaps in the curtains of the large window opposite the bed. I squint my eyes half-shut to protect them from the brightness, still not quite ready for the light of day yet.

I glance around, half-expecting to see Zach asleep, on the pillow next to me. It will be the first time I've woken up next to a man. But it is empty. I'm alone. I wonder where he is and what time it is. I have no clue, my phone is low on battery, and no clocks are on the walls.

I peel myself out of bed, put my charger into my phone, and head to my luggage to grab some clothes. Kicking off what I was wearing as I walk to the en-suite bathroom. The sight of my naked body in the bathroom mirror makes me flush. I think of Zach seeing me like this. Then I remember what I did last night right there in his bed and how the idea of him looking at my pussy turns me on so much I came in record time.

Quickly, I shower, get dressed, and pull my charger out of the socket. I can see that my sister has called once and Molly has called thirteen times. A lot of people come and go when you have the kind of cash that my family does, but Molly has always stuck around and never asked for a thing from me. When she heard about my father, she practically moved in for a few days to help me with the funeral arrangements. I send her a quick text since it's too early to call her now. She likes to sleep in on Saturday mornings.

Sticking the phone into my purse, I wander out of the room. The long corridors are deserted and I meet no one on my way down the grand curving stairs. It would be so easy for me to get lost if I wasn't keeping my wits about me, and frankly, even as it is, I feel distracted and a little off-balance.

I know my body is looking for Zach. He feels like an anchor in this enormous place. I need to call Molly when I get the chance. She will ground me.

"Good morning, Miss Johnson." a voice calls to me as I reach the bottom of the stairs.

I'm startled and glance around to see Arnold looking over at me from a set of wide double doors. "Oh, good morning to you too."

"Can I show you to the breakfast room?"

"Uh no," I reply, wrapping my arms around myself protectively. "I was just wondering where Zach is?"

"He's at work," Arnold explains.

I raise my eyebrows. "It's Saturday."

"Mr. Black has been known to even work on Sundays," Arnold replies gently, with the faintest flicker of a smile.

I run my hands through my hair. If he isn't around it might be my best opportunity to meet up with Molly. "Oh, I think I want to go out and get something to eat. Do I call a driver? Is there a car, or...?"

"Mr. Black did leave these for you," Arnold replies, dipping his fingers into his jacket packet and holding out a set of keys in my direction.

I stare at them for a moment. *Did he really...?*

"Thank you," I say, taking the keys from him. I glance down at them, and see a Porsche keyring dangling from the chain. My eyebrows shoot up. There is no way in hell he actually got me a car this fancy.

"It's one of his fleet," Arnold explains, noticing my surprise. "He said you are to use it as long as you're here."

"I've never driven one," I confess.

"I think you'll find that it is one of the easiest cars to drive." He drops his voice to a whisper. "And it's automatic."

I grin. "Is it insured?"

He grins back. "If you like I can show you how it all works."

"Yes, please!" I say enthusiastically. I might not know much about cars, but I know for damn sure that a Porsche is one of the best in the business. The kind of thing that my father would have deemed as too dangerous for my sister and me to ever drive. On my eighteenth birthday, I received my first car, a Fiat. Second hand, because my father said, I was bound to knock it about, and soon afterward Dad fell ill. A new car was the last thing I thought about.

Now, I am about to get to play with a Porsche and I'm already feeling excited about the prospect.

Arnold leads me out to a massive garage at the back of the house, and I am practically skipping on the spot as I follow him. We walk past an Aston Martin, a Rolls Royce, and a Lambo and I can't believe this is really happening. It feels crazy, but in the best possible way. And I am touched, to be honest, that Zach has already given enough thought to my needs when he is not around.

It could be as simple as the fact that he doesn't want to have to worry about calling his driver for me every time I want to go to the shops, but even so, this is above and beyond anything I expected. Maybe he's a little more thoughtful than I initially believed. Or maybe, I'm getting special gifts because I made out with him a little last night.

We stop next to a car with a dust cover on it.

When Arnold whisks it off, I swear my jaw nearly hits the floor. "This is the car?" I exclaim happily. "This one? Right here!"

It is bright red and seems to glow with barely-contained energy as it sits there in front of me. I run my hand over the glossy bonnet as I move around it. Inside, the seats are soft, supple cream leather, and I feel a shiver of excitement run down my spine at the way my life has suddenly changed in the space of a few days.

"Yes, this one, right here," Arnold replies with a slight chuckle. He seems amused by my excitement.

"Thank you, Arnold," I tell him after he shows me all the controls of car that will be mine for the duration of my time here.

"I'll leave you two to get to know each other," he tells me, and backs off to give me some time with the car.

I barely notice him going; my eyes are fixed on this thing that I'm already half-obsessed with. Maybe I'm more of a car person than I gave myself credit for. Or perhaps this is just the prettiest car I've ever seen in my entire life.

I feel all fuzzy and warm inside, and I know it has to do with more than just the car. It's the thought of seeing Zach this evening, when he gets back from work, and finding some way to thank him for his generosity.

I climb inside and wrap my fingers around the wheel. God, this is going to be so much fun to drive. I'd only been planning on heading into town for something to eat, but suddenly I feel the urge to go further. I would love to take her out for a real spin. Here I am, already giving her a gender. She is for sure a, her. She feels feminine and I kinda love her already. I know exactly where I am going to take her to.

Molly.

CHAPTER 13

SCARLETT

Molly still doesn't know about anything that has gone on between Zach and I. And there's a darn good reason for that. I know she would tell me I'm being crazy and that I am just asking for trouble getting involved with a man like Zach, even if it is just for business. She would have tried to talk me out of it, but at the time... I knew what I must do. I made promises to Mom and no matter what... I plan to keep my promise.

I pull out my phone and dial her number.

The phone rings a couple of times before Molly answers with a yawn, "Hey," she says sleepily. Molly likes to hit the town and party whenever she gets the chance, and there is a fifty-fifty likelihood that she is speaking to me from the bed of a random hook-up from last night. Molly works at a coffee shop, as a barista and she constantly has these guys who come in over and over again because they develop crushes on her that they can't shake off.

It doesn't surprise me; she always has such effervescent

energy, like she is about to overflow and pop at any second. People always seem fascinated by her. Out of the two of us, I am more shy and retiring. That said though, she could probably make a pop star seem shy and retiring while standing next to her.

"Hey," I say cautiously. "You got a minute to speak?"

"Of course, I do," she assures me. "In fact, if you hadn't called, I would have been late for my shift at work, so thanks."

"Oh, you're going to work on Saturday?" I ask, a little deflated.

"Yeah, not all of us can just laze around in our mansions all day," she teases. Then she laughs and explains that she is taking someone's lunch shift today.

"Right, because I have something to tell you," I reply, and I take a deep breath.

"Scarlett? What's going on?" she demands dramatically.

I consider if I should I just come right out and tell her? She's going to think I'm crazy anyway, but she's my best friend, and if anyone can help me navigate the mess I have gotten myself into in the quest to saving my family home, then it's going to be her.

I launch into the whole story. From the reading of the will, to getting slapped by Victoria, to meeting Zachary, to coming here, and moving in. I decide to leave out what happened the night before, when he kissed me. I think I didn't completely trust her not to come swooping in and try to save me from the black-hearted businessman.

"Oh, my God," she says breathlessly as soon as I am done. "Your—your dad really left the house to that bitch?"

"Yeah." I sigh. "I still can't believe it myself. Can't believe he would have done something like that. He knew how important the house was to Mom. How much she wanted it to stay with her girls."

"That is very weird," she mutters in agreement. "He knew that the two of you...anyway, that doesn't matter. What matters is—"

"That I'm going to fake-marry this guy to get my home back?" I finish up for her. "Yeah, trust me, I know it."

"I've heard some pretty crazy shit in my time, but this is too much even for me," she replies. "Are you okay? Are you out there now?"

"Yeah, I'm okay," I assure her. "And yes, I'm out here right now. I, uh...actually, I'm sitting in the car he gave me."

"He gave you a car?"

She screams this so loudly I have to pull the phone away from my ear to avoid blowing out an eardrum. "Yup," I confirm, my fingers stroking the luxurious leather seat.

"Seriously? That's crazy!"

"And it's a Porsche," I continue, knowing that I am boasting a little and struggling to care. She's always been more into vehicles than I have, and knowing that I am sitting in this thing must be driving her a little crazy. "And yes, before you ask, you can drive it," I promise.

"Good, because I was just going to steal it from you if you

didn't let me," she shoots back playfully. She then falls silent for a moment.

Yes, I can tell that she is still concerned. She has a right to be, everything I've told her would be setting off any sane person's alarm bells.

"Are you sure about this, Scarlett?" she asks gently. "I mean, I've been around this town enough to know that Zach has a serious reputation..."

"Yeah, I'm sure. I'm going to be fine, Molly. This is what I want to do." I shift in my seat and hope she can't feel the doubt in my heart. "We already agreed. The marriage is just in name only. I get the house and he gets the shares."

"And you believe him?"

I pause for a moment, remembering the way his mouth felt on mine, how it made me feel when he touched my cheek back in his office. As though bolts of lightning were running between us, a fiery energy barely contained.

"Scarlett?"

"Oh? Uh, yeah. Ernest took a look at the contract and he said it was all above board," I reply, evading the real question.

"I'm not talking about the pre-nup," she says patiently.

"Don't worry, Molly. I can take care of myself. He's just a guy, right?"

For a couple of seconds she goes completely silent and I know she's biting her tongue. "That's the spirit," she says finally, her voice extra bright. "So when are you going to come down and show me that car in person?"

"I'll come pick you up from work in it if you want?" I laugh.

"Great. I get off at three, I'll see you then?"

"See you then." I hang up and place both my hands on the wheel. A rush of energy moves through me, and I know at once, what I want to do with the rest of the day. I know it might be the stupidest idea I've ever had. In fact, it might even be tempting fate, but I'm not going to be able to get it out of my head until I give it a try, one way or the other. I push the keys into the slot and pull out of the garage, a smile on my face. There's someone I want to see and I'm not going to wait a minute longer to be with him again.

CHAPTER 14

SCARLETT

I fluff my hair in the mirror of the Porsche, and hope I can pass for the kind of sophisticated woman who Zach Black might actually look at twice. I dig through my purse pockets, find some lip-gloss and slick it on lips. My mouth becomes shiny and wet, hopefully, just what he's looking for. I don't know what it is, the kiss, the car, or something else entirely, but I can feel confidence oozing from me and I like it.

He sure knew what he was doing to me in that bedroom, leaving me so desperate for more that I'm willing to turn up at his work in the middle of the day to get it. Maybe he will be taken aback by my boldness, but then again every modern woman takes control of her sexuality. I mean, look at Molly. She goes out and takes what she wants and why not? We only live once, might as well enjoy it.

There's no way for him to know that I'm a virgin and I don't even know what I'm planning to do to him when I go in there, but I'll play it by ear. I'll be like one of those experienced women who turn up at their lover's offices and have sex on the desk.

The receptionist I met the last time is not at her desk. Instead, there is a homely looking woman. I give her the same spiel I gave the first receptionist. She ushers me towards the elevators. To my surprise, Dahlia is sitting at her desk. My first thought is why is she working on a Saturday? She must either love her work or Zack.

"Do you have an appointment?" she asks, eyeing me up and down, her eyes cold and hard.

I give her a haughty look. "I don't need one."

She shakes her head. "Mr. Black is busy right now." There is a barbed edge to her voice, as though she resents even having to take time out of her day to tell me this.

I cross my arms over my chest and narrow my eyes at her. I need to get into that office and see him, and I'm not going to let this woman get in the way of that. I reach into my pocket, pull out my phone, and dial his number. He answers a moment later.

"Scarlett?"

"Zack, could you please tell your secretary that your fiancée is here to see you?"

Dahlia's jaw drops. This definitely wasn't what she was expecting. She waves me through, giving me a bitter look, and that confirms my suspicion that she might have more than a little crush on Zack.

I push open his door, and there he is, sitting behind his desk.

He looks at me steadily, clearly pleased by my sudden arrival, but then his eyes trail up and down my body and a slow smile appears on his face.

I close the door behind me, turn around, and lock it. I feel a little giddy. I just want to make out with him again, the way we did yesterday, and I know I'm not going to be able to shake that from my head until we do. I need to get it out of my system. The sound of the lock is loud in the silence. Slowly, I turn around and lean against the door.

He says nothing, just watches me with those amazingly light eyes of his.

"You know, I think your secretary might have a crush on you," I tell him, as I push myself away from the door.

His eyes widen slightly. He is clearly trying to figure out what I am doing here dressed like this and acting like this.

His confusion gives me confidence.

I start making my way towards the desk, my gait slow and sure. I don't know where this version of me has come from, but I like her. She is confident, in-control, and cool in a way Scarlett isn't. His gaze is fixed on my legs. I'm wearing a short skirt, and I suppose I picked it out this morning for a reason, even if I wasn't aware of it then.

"You ever hook up with any of your staff?" I wonder aloud.

He shakes his head, his eyes never leaving me. "Not a chance. I don't need the trouble."

I come to a stop in front of his desk.

"Why? You jealous?" he asks, a smile flicking up his face.

I shrug. "No, but if we're going to sell this marriage thing to people, it'll be a lot easier to do if you're not hooked up with the people who work for you."

"We don't need to sell anything to anyone," he reminds me. "Just need to sign that certificate and its official."

"I suppose so," I agree.

He reaches into his pocket and pulls out a small velvet box. "Though if you need to sell it to anyone else..." He holds the box out to me.

With arched eyebrows, I take it from him, and pop it open. Inside, a ring with an enormous diamond sparkles up at me. "What's this?" I gasp.

"I thought it might make things a little more realistic," he explains, eyeing me.

I stare at it with fascination. Our family has great old pieces of jewelry at the bank, but I've never been allowed to wear jewelry like this. Dad was always paranoid about us being robbed. His theory was, he preferred his daughters with all their fingers intact. "Is it real?"

"Of course, it is."

"I can't take this." There's something about seeing the ring right on this royal blue velvet bed that makes me feel...I don't know, but certainly not right. Slipping this ring over my finger, would be giving myself to him in a deep way that I don't want to do. Not yet. Or do I?

"Why not?" he asks. "Sounds like you liked the car well enough."

"How did you know?"

"I'd recognize that car anywhere," he cuts me off as he motions over to the window.

The way he speaks to me, there's just so much confidence there. He doesn't care to play to my emotions, or say the PC thing. He says what he thinks and doesn't hold back. And so far, I like it.

Still, I'm not going to take the ring. It's far too expensive, not to mention the fact that my clumsy ass will probably lose it in five seconds flat. I hold it out to him, waiting for him to take it from me, but he doesn't move a muscle.

"It's insured."

"Even so," I mumble.

"Put it on," he orders softly, his eyes glittering like two precious stones.

I shake my head.

He comes around the desk. "Just to see what it looks like," he says persuasively, as he takes the box from me and pulls the ring out. Taking my hand, he slides it over my finger.

I watch, almost hypnotized by the strangeness of the act. I've imagined this moment before, of course I have, how it would feel when the man I would marry slips the ring onto my finger and makes it official. But never in these circumstances. Even so, there's something special in the moment, whether or not I want to admit it to myself. His nearness, the heat from his body, the scent of his aftershave…

"We need to hurry up and make this marriage official," I blurt out to kill the moment. I pull my gaze away from the ring and focus back on him.

He looks triumphant, as though he has got one over on me and he knows it.

I can feel the heat of a flush running up my neck, and I hate myself a little for being taken in so easily by just his touch.

"If it's about the wedding night, we don't actually have to wait," he replies, a twist to his sensual lips. The way he is looking at me is as if he wants to lean down and take a bite out of me.

I feel the heat between my legs starting to build and I try to ignore it. "It's not about that—it has nothing to do with…" I shrug. "It's so I can get started on the—on the land. I'm worried Victoria will sell it before we can stop her."

"The land, huh?" He lets his hand trail around my waist. "And that's why you came down here in the middle of the day? Because you wanted to make sure that the deal with the land was going to go through?"

Distracted by his hand, I am unable to form a reply.

He moves his mouth down to my neck and brushes his lips across my skin.

I practically swoon.

He knows just what I'm here for and he has no problem giving it to me. He slides his lips up along my neck, all the way up to my ear. "It's Saturday, Scarlet. You know, you could have just waited until I got home," he continues, tracing his tongue over the whorls of my ear. "But you wanted this, didn't you? You want me to do this..." He slides his hand down and between my legs.

I just forget entirely that we are in his office with people filling up the floors below us. Then there's Dahlia who probably has her ear to the door. Maybe I even want her to hear us, to prove to myself that this is actually happening. Zachary Winston Black is touching me. I'm not just imagining it.

CHAPTER 15

SCARLETT

His fingers travel up the inside of my thighs and trace over my panties.

I can't help the moan that escapes my mouth.

It seems like it was what he was waiting for. He grins as if satisfied with my reaction. "You're such a good girl, Scarlett," he purrs into my ear. "But you don't have to always be that good, you know. Sometimes it's nice to be a little bad..." He pushes his fingers beneath the fabric and caresses my pussy.

I gasp at just how good it feels. He loops an arm around my waist to keep me upright and I cling on to him for support, my knees already threatening to give out from underneath me.

"Look how wet and juicy you are," he says, his voice thick with lust.

I have long-since lost the power of words, but I hope the way I am moving my body back against his tells him everything he needs to know.

He catches my chin in his other hand and pulls my face around to look at him. "Do you want me to make you mine, Scarlett?"

I can't reply, my brain is too overheated to come up with anything but wordless desire for him, him, and more of him. I nod.

"Say it," he orders me.

"Yes—yes, I want you," I gasp.

That is all he needs to hear. He pushes my skirt up, exposing me completely. He then picks me up and places me on the desk. Just as he is about to kneel down between my legs, there is a knock at the door.

I freeze.

"Mr. Black?" Dahlia calls through the door. "There's someone on the—"

"Tell them I'll call them back," he cuts her off, his eyes never leaving mine.

"But—"

"I'll call them back," he repeats firmly, and with that, he hooks his fingers around my panties, pulls them down, and buries his mouth on my pussy.

The feeling is...well, it's beyond anything I have ever felt before in my life. His mouth is warm and it feels like he is tasting every inch of me at once. Before this, I'd tried to imagine what it might be like to have a man go down on me, but never in a million years did I think it would feel this damn *good*. His tongue flicks out over my clit, as though he has been waiting to get here since the moment he met me. I thought that men always just wanted penetration, but he lets out something between a groan and a growl of pleasure that tells me he is more than happy right here.

He seals his lips around my clit and begins to apply a light pleasure, going slow at first, letting me get used to the feel of his mouth on my pussy. I wonder if he knows that I've never done this before. I clamp my hands onto the edges of the desk and tip my head back, gasping for air.

"Fuck, you taste like heaven," he murmurs, as he slides his hands beneath my ass and pulls me closer towards him, as though he can't get enough of me.

I look down and watch the incredible sight of his dark head between my thighs eating me out like it is the only thing that matters to him in the world. He is so gorgeous, so sexy and so many women in this city would kill to be where I am at this moment, but he has chosen me. Me, alone.

I can already feel myself getting close

"Ah..." I gasp as the waves start rushing through my body. I close my eyes and savor the feeling. His tongue is soft but insistent, drawing circles around my clit, closing in on me, like he knows he is getting me there. His fingers dig into my ass and he moans again, the vibrations of the sound rushing up through me. Through the increasing waves of pleasure, I realize he is enjoying this as much as I am.

My body is crying out for the relief of an orgasm, and I am grinding my hips back against his face, my knuckles white from where I'm hanging on to the edges of the desk so hard... The fire that has been growing in my belly since he kissed me last night bursts, consuming me, like an inferno and I can't hold it in any longer.

"Fuck," I groan as the pressure in me finally releases. It pulses through me, lighting up my nervous system and turning my muscles to jelly. Zach doesn't move his mouth from my clit. His tongue is still flicking back and forth, until I push his head back. But the feeling of his stubble on my thighs is still lingering.

He rises to his feet and kisses me, hard, pushing his tongue into my mouth. The taste of my pussy on his tongue is the reminder of where he has just been.

He pulls back and cocks an eyebrow. "That was what you were looking for when you came in here today, wasn't it?"

I can still see my wetness glistening on his face. "Yes," I whisper, as I reach down to grab my panties, pull them up, and roll my skirt down over my hips. I can only hope Dahlia didn't hear the sounds I was making as he ate me out. My legs are trembling and I'm fairly confident they won't actually hold me up yet. They feel like matchsticks, ready to give out and snap beneath me if I put any weight on them. But I feel so exposed and vulnerable, I know I need to get out of here before I give myself completely away. "I have to go meet with my friend," I tell him, even though it's still a few hours before I said I would pick Molly up. I need a little space to clear my head.

Something glints in the corner of my eye, and I glance down to see the ring he put on my finger. It looks so pretty, and it fits perfectly, which is odd. How could he possibly know my ring size?

"Anything you say," he replies smoothly.

I can tell he can see right through me. He knows I'm getting out of here because I'm a coward. It is one thing to have him go down on me, but when it comes to giving him my virginity...yeah, I need a little time to think. And maybe some space with Molly to talk it out.

He flashes me a smile as he unlocks the door and pushes it open for me.

I see the look on Dahlia's face as I walk out.

She might not have heard much, but she seems to know what we were getting up to in there.

My pussy is still throbbing and swollen. I throw a smile in her direction,

She purses her lips at me with distaste. As the elevator takes me down to the ground floor, the memory of the look on her face lingers with me. She disapproves of me. And she's not afraid to show it.

Maybe she really does have a crush on him or something, but I've got no right to stick my nose in his affairs. What did he say to me? That he would let me know when he feels tired of me, so we could both move on. The thought of this really stings, even though I know I'm the one who set up those rules.

I climb back into the car. I already know I don't want this thing we have to just be over like that. What are the chances that I'm ever going to be in a position where an impossibly sexy guy wants me and knows how to make it incredible for me? So yeah, a lot of people might say I'm crazy to marry a man just to save a house. But maybe I'm not quite *that* crazy. I want him, he wants me, and I don't see why I shouldn't allow myself a little fun.

As I pull away from his office building, I know exactly where I'm going to go. I want to make sure that tonight is as perfect as it possibly can be. And I'm going to make sure that when I give my virginity away, I'm going to do everything right.

CHAPTER 16

ZACH

As soon as I walk through the door that evening, I know something is different. The whole place is quiet, the lights are dim, and Arnold is nowhere to be seen. He's usually right there to help with my bags and coat, asking about my day, but today… nothing. I put my briefcase down, take off my coat, and wonder if this has anything to do Scarlett and the little visit she made to my office.

God, that had been one of the hottest hook-ups I've done in years. I've never fooled around in my office before. I've never wanted a woman enough to interrupt my work, I guess, but being with her and seeing the reluctant way that she gave herself to me, as though she knew there was no way she could resist. That has to be some of the hottest shit I've ever seen in my life. Hearing her moan and cry out in pleasure, as I tasted her sugar-sweet peach for the first time did something to me. I can still taste her on my tongue.

I know I'm not going to be able to rest until I have her.

I make my way up to the bedroom, taking the stairs two at a

time, hoping I'm going to find what I think I'm going to. I push open my bedroom door.

And there she is.

Laid out on my bed, looking like a fantasy brought to reality. Her long fair hair is draped around her, and she is wearing pure white lingerie, the kind that a bride might wear on her wedding night. Her eyes are wide as she sits up and starts to crawl across the bed towards me.

Unbuttoning my shirt, I start walking towards her.

She stops at the edge on her hands and knees, unable to look up and meet my eyes. "I hope you don't mind. I gave your staff the night off," she whispers, staring straight ahead at some point on the wall behind me.

I fling away my shirt, put my finger under her chin, and tip her head up to face me. I watch as her soft lips part like a cut peach at my touch. "They're your staff now too."

"Zach, I have to tell you something," she murmurs. "I'm...I've never done this before. I'm a, you know..."

It's not exactly a surprise. Even though she seems particularly receptive to my touches, there's something innocent and tentative about her that has already tipped me off.

She bites her lips, gazing up at me, waiting for me to respond, like she fears that I'm going to turn her down or something.

I hide a smile of triumph. The idea that no other man has been inside her excites me, fills me with possessive pride. And here I was thinking I was doing Simon's daughter a favor..."And you want me to be the first?" I ask softly.

She nods. "More than anything."

I'll make her take me inside that sweet little pussy of hers and I'll fuck her until she screams for more. I lean down and take her sweet innocent mouth. She moans as I part her lips with my tongue, coaxing her open, getting her to open up to me. I quickly pull off my jacket and shirt then toss them aside while still claiming her delicious mouth. Parting our mouths long enough to climb on the bed and push her so I can lay on top of her, sliding my hands up her arms and guiding them over her head.

"You have no idea how long I've wanted you like this," I breathe into her ear.

She moans, lifting her hips so she can grind her body against mine.

Her movements are uncertain, but everything she's doing is turning me on. I reach down between her legs and trace my fingers over her panties, feeling the warmth and the wetness of her through the fabric. "I'm going to make this pussy mine," I tell her.

Scarlett moans again.

How long has she been waiting for me like this? Long enough that she is soaking wet. I slip my fingers beneath her panties and find her honeyed hole. She lets out a gasp as I push a finger inside her, and then another. She is so soaked my finger makes a squelching sound. "God, you feel so fucking good," I murmur.

I feel her fingers sink into my back as she gets used to the feeling of my plunging inside of her. I want this to be as good for her as I know it's going to be for me, and that means taking my time, not that taking my time exploring this gorgeous body is going to be hard work. I lean down and push aside the lacy cup covering one of her breasts, the flimsy material making way for me at once. I take the exposed nipple between my lips and suck it softly, until I feel it swelling to a hard tip between my lips. I add a third finger and get her used to the sensation of being taken like this.

As she moans, my fingers slowly work further and further inside of her.

When I move to her other breast, I feel her fingers push through my hair, guiding me to where she wants me to be. That is a good sign. I know that first-timers can be nervous, too nervous to actually say what they want, but she is letting me know what she needs from me and I am only too happy to give it to her. I could eat her pussy every day for the rest of my life.

Her breath is coming faster now, and I can tell she is edging closer. I want to be inside her, but I am willing to wait as long as it takes until she catches up with me. My cock is so hard it aches, but I know the wait will be worth it. My head fills, all at once, with the thoughts of everything that I can teach her, once we have gotten this first time out of the way, and I know right then that this is going to be seriously fun.

I push her thighs apart then yanking aside the crotch of her panties, I feast on her sweet flesh until she comes, screaming, her hands clawing my arms, her thighs clamping around my head. Her juices fill my mouth and pour down my throat. With admirable dedication, I lick her clean. Only when her breathing calms down do I lift my head.

"I want you to fuck me now. I'm ready," she breathes.

"Are you sure? I'm bigger than average and it's going to hurt," I murmur.

"I'm sure," she replies.

I look into those outrageously beautiful brown eyes. They are filled with lust and want, all aimed at me, and I know I'm going to come so hard— I'm going to see fucking stars.

I undress her slowly, peeling off the rest of the lingerie and exposing her perfect, curvy body, inch by gorgeous inch. Then I loosen my belt and take off my pants.

Curiously, she pushes herself up on her elbows, and lets her eyes rove down my mostly nude body.

I've had plenty of women look at me with lust before, but the way she gazes at me is something else entirely, as if she has never seen anything like me in her life.

When I pull off my boxers and my cock springs free, she lets out a little gasp. "Jesus, it's so big," she murmurs, watching as I roll a condom over my cock.

"Don't worry, you can take it," I promise. "I'll make it feel good..." I push her back on the bed and part her legs. She wraps her arms around me, her fingers trailing over my back, and I look deep into her eyes as I slowly push myself into her for the first time.

She is so tight I almost come right there, but she lets out a cry of pain, which makes me lose some of my intense excitement. "Shhh...it'll only hurt for a minute," I whisper, but I know I'm massive, so I stop and allow her pussy to flex and spread around my cock. I press my head into her shoulder, letting out a groan of want for her. I have been inside first-timers before, of course, but never one who felt like this to me. The thought of her, waiting all this time for the right person to come along, and then for her to decide that the right person just so happened to be me...yeah, it didn't get much better than this.

"Better?" I ask.

She nods.

I push in deep.

"Oh..." she cries out with a moan, her eyes widening, as I slowly slide my cock inside her until I am buried balls deep to the hilt within her.

I turn to kiss her softly, not moving for a moment to let her get used to the feeling of me inside her. "Are you ok?" I ask.

"Amazing," she breathes, and she pushes her hips forward to take me even deeper.

The sight of her wriggling her little hips trying to take more of me inside her is more than I can take. I feel myself losing control and I have to start thinking of a particularly irritating salesman I know. It ruins it for me, but goddamn it, I want this sweetness to last. I begin to move, thrusting harder, building up a pace inside of her, and she does her best to keep up.

Soon, we are moving together as though there is no space between us at all. She winds her arms tight around me and clings. I don't want this to be over. It's not just the incredible way it feels. It's the sounds she makes, the feel of her ragged breath on my neck is too hot and too good. I've secretly wanted and been denied this woman for so long and now, she is all mine. She belongs to me. She's given something to me that no other man will ever have, and that is about the sexiest thing I can possibly imagine.

She tentatively hooks her ankles behind my back, drawing me in deeper, and even she seems surprised by her eagerness to have me fill her up. I thought she might struggle a little to take all of me inside her, but she's wet enough and eager enough. It's as though she has been waiting for this forever too.

"Oh my God," she gasps.

I can see the glaze in her eyes that tells me she is getting close again. I want her to come with me inside of her. I want to feel her pussy tighten around my cock. I lower my mouth to her ear again. "Come for me, Scarlett," I order.

That's all she seems to need to push her over the edge.

I feel her body give out beneath me, her entire being quivering in my arms as she finally goes over. Her pussy clenching hard around me, over and over again. I hold myself still inside of her and let her massage my cock from the inside out. Her moans flow into each other, soft and sweet, like this is the release she has been waiting for as long as she can remember. It doesn't take long till I am right there with her, my cock spurting my seed.

I wish I could taste her orgasm again. I wish we could have gone bareback, but we can save that for next time. *Next time.* It's not often that I'm still inside a woman as I'm thinking about what the next time will be like with her...

When I pull myself out, she grasps my head and kisses me again, like she's not ready for this to be over. I know how she feels. I feel so protective of her right now. I never feel this way about a woman I've just had sex with. When I collapse on the bed next to her while catching my breath, I glance over to see her gazing at me. I reach out and touch her soft cheek. Our eyes lock and something passes between us. A secret language that only our bodies recognize. That has never happened to me before.

"That was..." she murmurs, then shakes her head and giggles. "See, it was so good, I don't even have the words to talk about it." Satiated and well-fucked, her hair a mess all over the pillow, and her make-up slightly smudged she still manages to look like a little golden angel.

"You don't need to talk about it," I drawl suggestively. "You can just show me, right?"

And that is exactly what she does.

CHAPTER 17

SCARLETT

"Uh...what's different about you?" Molly asks as soon as I walk through the door of the cute coffee shop she works at.

I beam at her before I go find a table for us. I sort of knew she would be able to tell. I feel as though I am walking a little taller, exuding some of the confidence and charisma that is usually reserved for her.

She joins me at the table, bringing us both a coffee, and cocks her head at me. "Hmmm." She taps her finger on her chin. "What's going on with you, Scarlett?"

I bite my lip. I don't even know where to start. I want to tell her everything. I know she is going to lose her mind since she's been telling me for ages I should just find someone to do it with, someone who wasn't too crazy and had a reputation for being good in the sack. Well, now I have, but I'm not sure how she's going to react to the fact that it's Zach. In her opinion, I should not get too attached to him. People like him go in and out of people's lives just for the fun of it. She said she understood him better than me, because she's like that too.

But she is my best friend, and I need someone to talk about it with. "I had sex," I blurt out.

Her eyebrows practically shoot off the top of her head. For a few seconds, she is too shocked to talk. Then... "You did what!" she exclaims so loudly all the people at the tables around us turn their heads in our direction.

I shush her, but giggle a little to myself. She is so expressive and passionate about everything, it's one of the reasons I love her so much. "I had sex," I repeat, lowering my voice this time just in case anyone else has decided that our conversation sounds more interesting than theirs.

"With who?" she asks, eyes wide.

"Zach," I reply.

Her jaw drops. "No *way*," she gasps. "You have to be shitting me, right? You didn't...not with him?"

"Yeah, I did," I admit. "And it was amazing, seriously. I didn't think it would be, what with it being my first time and all, but he was...oh, Molly, he was awesome. So gentle and it was so good! He's so sexy. We ended up having sex all weekend long. I mean, I could hardly walk straight this morning."

"I can't believe that I'm hearing this," she says in an awed voice while shaking her head. "I mean, I knew you thought he was hot, but..."

"You did?"

"Oh, come on, I'm not blind, deaf, and dumb," she teases. "It was written all over your face whenever you mentioned seeing him at parties. And when he gave you the car, you were practically giddy when you came and picked me up in it."

"Wow, I didn't realize I was being so transparent."

She laughs and reaches over to squeeze my hand. "I actually think it's kind of cute," she replies. "You're obviously into him, and now...well, I'm not going to go for the obvious, and quote the, 'he got into you' joke, but you know."

I laugh. I'm glad I chose to come out here today. I'd planned on just staying in and doing some reading while I waited for him to get home, so we could fool around again, but it's good I came out. I need to get out into the real world and see people.

"He sure got into me," I say with a wide grin. It's wild, saying it out loud to someone else. I wasn't even sure it was real, felt more like a dream, but now since someone else knows, it's real. I feel giddy, overexcited. Like I am on the brink of bursting.

She takes a sip of her coffee.

I look down at my cup. I've almost forgotten about mine in the thrill of confessing to her.

Suddenly, she hits me with a hard stare.

"What?" I ask, shifting in my seat. I know that look. It's the look she gives me when she's worried I am about to do something that's counter to my best interests.

She hesitates for a moment before she comes out with it, "It *is* just sex for you, right? I mean, you're not getting attached to him, or anything like that, are you?"

"No!" I reply at once, but then I shrug. "Well, I mean, I live in his house. And we do share the same favorite book. And I guess..."

"Okay, I'm going to stop you right there..." She raises her palm and her expression is serious. "You need to remember that this guy isn't *actually* your husband."

"Well, yeah, I know that," I say defensively, but the lines are becoming blurred.

"And he's not ever going to be," she continues quickly.

I nod, but something inside of me feels defiant. I don't want her to ruin it.

"You agreed on this as part of a business deal," she continues undisturbed by my falling face, "not as some romance of the century. Don't go and lose it, babe. Everyone tells you there's something special there or that there should be...but it can just be sex. Really. You just have to keep in your head that it's just chemistry."

I lean back in my seat and stare at her. I know that she's right, and I also know that she's raining on my little happiness parade.

"I'm glad you're no longer around your evil stepmother and she isn't corrupting you with poison apples or something, but Zach is not your Prince Charming. You know what I'm saying?"

I shift in my seat. I want to tell her that of *course* I know what she's talking about, I'm a grown woman who knows how this stuff works, but she knows as well as I do that it would be a straight-up lie. I've never done anything like this before, and I guess that makes me vulnerable to misreading signals and assuming things about a relationship that aren't true. "Yeah, I get it," I agree, but I'm already slightly regretting telling her about Zach and me. I wish I could take it back and go back to the time where I could convince myself there is something between us.

She smiles gently at me. "I'm only telling you this because I know my girl can do a million times better than Zach Black."

"You better not say that to anyone at the wedding, they're not going to be too impressed..."

"I won't say it to anyone, but I see much bigger and better men in your future. Trust me, I know these things."

"Right," I agree, and I manage a smile. Then I hide behind my coffee cup, hoping that it's enough to keep the doubt on my face concealed. Because, even though I know she is right, that getting involved with a man like Zach for anything other than the pure physical would be a bad idea...I still find my stomach all a flutter when I think of him. And for the life of me, I cannot imagine any man better than Zach. Even if I turned into a vampire and lived for a million years.

"Anyway, what's been going on with you?" I ask, quickly shifting the conversation back to her.

And with that, the conversation about my sex life is dropped and we get on to hers, but her words tick away at the back of my mind for the rest of our meeting together, until I can hardly stop thinking about ways to prove her wrong.

Which is crazy. I know that it doesn't make any sense to prove her wrong, and yet, still, I feel the urge. As we talk, I begin to form a plan in my head. And soon enough, I have secured something that I am confident will make my point. Once and for all.

I head back down to Zach's office as soon as I'm done visiting with Molly. I march up to his office right away. Dahlia gets to her feet and steps out in front of me before I can go inside, and I fight the urge to roll my eyes at her.

"He doesn't have time to see you right now," she tells me.

I could swear there is a slight sneer to her voice. "I don't need him for long," I reply, and brush past her, not giving her the chance to so much as try it with me. I push open his door and step inside, and I am glad to see that he's in there by himself.

I close the door behind me, lock it, and he glances up at me from whatever document he'd been reading...and the rest of the world drops away.

CHAPTER 18

SCARLETT

"What's wrong Scarlett?" he asks with a frown. Then he sees the look in my eyes and I guess it clicks into place for him, because he gets to his feet and makes his way around the desk towards me.

I feel a little breathless. Am I really going to do this? Molly's words rotate around my head: *It can just be sex.* Well, if that's all it is, then I want to enjoy every inch of it that I can, while I still can. While he still belongs to me.

I bite my lip, as he gets closer; I swear, just the look in his eyes sometimes is enough to make my body ache for him. When he meets my gaze and I can tell that he wants me too, I feel like someone has set me on fire, burning up from the inside out. He must know what he is capable of doing to me.

I wonder, for a second, how many other women he has made feel this way, then push that painful thought away quickly. That's not important. What *is* important is the fact that he wants me now. Me. So what if it might not last forever.

He plants his hands on the door, either side of me, pinning

me to the spot, and his gaze trails down to my lips, slowly. He moves in and kisses me, taking his time, parting my lips with his tongue and moving it against mine, testing me, teasing me. When his tongue slips into my mouth I start to suck it, and feel whatever resolve I'd been hanging on to turn to jelly inside me. It's impossible to have any doubts when he just makes it so damn easy to believe that this is… that this *has* to be something more.

He pushes his hand under my skirt, rolling it up and over my hips, grasping at the flesh beneath. I groan, not caring if anyone outside the door - basically, the witch Dahlia - hears me. In fact, maybe there is just some small part of me that hopes she does. I want the world to know I am his and he is mine. To know that nobody else is allowed near him.

Not fucking Dahlia….not anyone!

"Go bend over my desk," he breathes in my ear, and he swings me around.

I walk with unsteady steps to the desk. I am facing a giant window that looks out over the whole city below. An entire world, moving on as normal, and here we are about to have sex in the middle of the day, like animals who cannot get enough of one another.

He rolls up my skirt quickly, and I moan as he pulls my panties down. It's crazy. It's wanton. It's shameless. It's lustful, but I don't care. I want him. I need him. If I don't feel him inside me in the next two seconds, I feel as if I might explode.

He is quick to oblige. I hear the tear of a condom, and briefly wonder if he just keeps them around for moments like this one. Before the thought becomes ugly, I feel him pressing against my slit and my minds blanks out as I release a groan of pleasure.

He plants a hand on the small of my back to keep me steady as he pushes inside of me. I gasp and clutch a hold of the desk for support as he enters me. I'd been told, way back when, that when a man has a very big cock the most painful position is from the back, but I haven't found that with him, not once. No, if anything, the pleasure is always so intense I feel as if I am going to pass out.

"Fuck, how is it that you're still so tight?" he growls, as he pushes all the way inside me.

This new angle takes me by surprise; it feels so good, my pussy clamps tight around his cock, and I can see from his reflection in the window beyond me that it feels just the same way for him, too. I know he's savoring the feeling of me around him.

He begins to move inside of me, going in long, slow strokes at first, and I get lost to the way it feels. He knows just what he is doing, just how to touch me, just how to make me his. Ever since we first had sex, I've been a little mad at myself that I waited as long as I did to give myself this intense pleasure, but then, I remind myself also that not every guy is going to be as good as he is. I got lucky with my first time and now, I want to make it a tenth time, twentieth, hundredth.

He slides his hand between my legs and begins to play with my clit as he moves inside me. The sensations spread out all across my body, as I tip my head back and moan. I feel his hand working into my hair, tugging my head back just slightly.

"Look at me," he orders, his voice low, leaving no room for argument.

I open my eyes and catch his gaze. It is so laden with want for me that I almost come right then and there. "Oh..." I groan, and I begin to move back against him, pushing my hips into his groin so that he can fill me balls deep. Every time he is inside me, all I want to do is submit to him completely. His fingers are soft on my clit where his dick is hard inside of me, and the contrast has me building quickly. I know that I can't hold off much longer. I press my lips together to keep any sound from escaping my mouth...and then I remember Dahlia outside and I don't want to keep it in. I don't care who hears me. I want the whole office to know that this man is mine.

All mine.

"Ah!" I cry out, as the feeling washes through me. My legs shudder and I grasp the desk for dear life. I can barely manage to keep upright. He moves inside me once, twice, three times more, and then I feel him find his own release, too. He lets out a deep, throaty growl that seems to rise from somewhere primal inside of him, and I am proud that I am the one who drew it out of him. His cock twitches and jerks as he finishes inside me.

My legs are trembling and my breath is coming quickly. I can still feel the shockwaves of pleasure pulsing through my body from what he has just done to me.

"You okay?" he asks.

Everything is still so new, my body still so sensitive to every single touch. I hope it stays that way forever. I hope I never get tired of this, not with him. This is too sweet, too power-ful, too much to ever want to give up...

With a frown, I push those thoughts to the back of my mind. This isn't what this is about. I came here to prove that I could have sex with him and have it mean nothing at all but plea-sure. Letting myself go down that rabbit hole is not going to make my point. "I'm fine," I assure him.

He grins and offers me a hand to help me up.

"I guess I should let you get back to work," I tell him, as I rearrange my clothes and get myself back to some semblance of decency once more. I know that when I step outside, I am going to be getting the stink-eye from his secretary, but it's hard to care when my whole body feels like a walking ball of endorphins.

"I guess you should," he replies, but he grabs my hand, pulls me to him, and kisses me once more.

It's the kind of kiss that takes your breath away. The kind of kiss that could make a girl believe that there is really some-thing here. I linger, savoring it for just a moment longer, and then I pull away. "I should—I should get going," I mumble, the heat rising through my cheeks. I need to get out of here before he has me on the desk again.

"See you back home," he says.

I smile at him before I head to the door. I don't want to go, but I know I need to get out of here if I'm going to keep a hold of what remains of my sanity. I push the door open, ignore the dirty look that Dahlia is giving me on the other side, make my way out of his office and back down to my car.

My legs are a little wobbly, but they can still carry me. Just like my brain is a little fuzzy around the edges, but I recognize that Molly is right. I need to make sure I keep things between us purely surface-level if I don't want to get wrapped up in something from which I can't escape.

CHAPTER 19

ZACH

"**G**ood morning, Mr. Black!"

"Morning, Dahlia." I usually wouldn't bother to look up from the papers I flick through as I drink my coffee, but something in her voice draws my attention this particular morning. My eyebrows rise up when I see the look she's sporting.

I don't give much of a damn about what my staff wear to work as long as they get the job done the way they're supposed to, but this is taking it a little too far. Dahlia is wearing a strappy top that pushes her breasts up and there is a ridiculous amount of cleavage on show, and a black skirt that is so short, it reveals the darker material of her stockings underneath. Her hair is loose around her shoulders and she is wearing bright-red lipstick. She looks as though she is ready to hit the club for a night out, not spend the day answering my emails and organizing my meetings.

She has never dressed like this before though, and she's been working for me for a good few years at this point. I can't figure out why she would have bothered to put on such an outfit this far into the game. Unless...

My mind flashes back to what happened yesterday. Scarlett had just marched in here and the two of us...well, if Dahlia was going to start getting jealous about anything, it would have been what we did in the office when I should have been working, that's for sure. Maybe it has something to do with that.

She notices me noticing her, and pushes her chest forward, as though she is waiting for me to offer a comment on the way she looks.

I decide it's safer for me not to say a thing and hope that this new style she has adopted dies out soon.

"Can I get you anything, Mr. Black?" she asks, smiling brightly. Her lipstick is so red, I swear her teeth look whiter than usual.

I shake my head. "Just make sure that you mail my schedule through to Brian for Wednesday, and I'll let you know if there's anything else I need from you."

She runs her hands over her hips and offers me a wide-eyed stare that I assume she believes is laced with meaning. "If there's *anything* at all that I can do for you," she says huskily. "You just let me know, all right?"

"All right," I say.

"See you soon," she calls flirtatiously, as she pulls the door shut behind her.

I put my coffee cup down on the table. What the hell is that about? If she does any more of this, I'm going to have to sit her down and ask her to stop this nonsense or get HR to straighten her out.

It's not that she's never shown any interest in me before. I'm not blind. I can tell when she's checking me out or when she's hoping that I'm going to shoot a look in her direction. If that's what she wants from me, she should never have come to work for me, because I don't go near shit like that. Fucking where I work, is like shitting where I eat as far as I'm concerned.

But she's always been subtle. At the moment, she is essentially laying herself out on a silver platter for me. She has no chance, even if I didn't believe in mixing business with pleasure. There is only one woman on my mind, one woman who matters, and that is Scarlett.

And this thought just hit me like a pinch to my solar plexus.

I lean back in my chair and stare at the closed door incredulously. *Goddamnit. How did that happen?* I really thought I would be able to keep myself separate from any feelings, anything real. I'd been doing it for years after all.

But I know she's not just any woman. She's the woman I agreed to marry. Of course, she believes the bullshit that I'm marrying her for the shares, but I can't hide from the truth. Those shares are nothing to me. I make and lose shares like that in a day without blinking an eye. And even if I did marry her for the shares I could have played this off without her moving in with me, but I didn't want to do that... did I? No, I wanted her near me, close to me, in my house, where I could see her all the time. I'd arranged it in such a way to make sure that she would be close to me, no matter what.

My skin is prickling with this new realization.

Dahlia is out there, dressed up all hot and pretty, trying to look like the most fuckable woman on the planet, and I can't even give her a second thought. Hell, I can confidently say there isn't another woman alive I want. Even now, coming directly from her warm body, all I can think about is how much I want to be with her again. To see her smile, to take in the look on her face when she laughs. To touch her body, push her hair back from her face and look into her eyes as I hold her.

I remember what her father said to me, what feels like a few lifetimes ago now—that I should stay away from his daughter. I had thought then that it was because he believed I was bad news for his daughter. But maybe, just maybe—he had been able to tell she would be equally bad news for me.

CHAPTER 20

SCARLETT

I hum to myself as I stroll down the high street. The breeze is in my hair and I'm feeling like I am walking on air. It's a bright, sunny day, and everything feels as though it is finally falling into place.

I decided earlier this morning I wanted a day to myself, just wandering around the shops, taking in the city. I've been so distracted with discovering my sexuality that it's been easy to forget everything else I'm missing out on. Then I meet Lori for lunch.

"He gave you a Porsche?" she gasps.

I nod and laugh. "Yeah, he did..."

"So what are you doing hanging around here? If I had a car, you wouldn't see me for dust. I'd be off on road-trips all the time," she remarks with a long, wistful sigh. "Can you imagine how much fun that would be?"

"Yeah, well, I don't really have time for road trips," I reply automatically.

She raises her eyebrows. "Don't you?"

I opened my mouth to protest, but closed it again. I'd been so used to just running around trying to keep everything in check, but now I didn't have to do anything anymore. "I guess you're right," I concede. "But I don't know if there's anywhere I want to take the car..."

"I know. I'll take care of the car for you," she assures me with a broad smile. "You just go out and have some fun, yeah? Take some time for yourself. Relax with Zach."

"This all sounds like a scheme to get your hands on the car." I raise a brow at her.

She shakes her head vigorously. "I just want what's best for you," she adds earnestly.

I can see the twinkle in her eyes. I know what she is thinking. I decide it is best just to hand over the keys to her and save us both the hassle of pretending she isn't going to sneak it out on a ride as soon as I went out the door.

"Just be careful with it, all right?" I warn.

"Don't you know? There's a special place in hell for people who hurt Porches," she shot back with a big grin.

I smile back at her. She has her license, so I'm not worried.

"I will..."

I figure also that the rest of her advice is probably good, too. I know she just gave it me to get what she wants, but I haven't had any time to myself from the time Dad fell sick, or actually since Mom got cancer. Besides a woman getting married to a man like Zach, should live a life of sheer leisure, shouldn't she?

I'm not sure what I'm going to do with myself after this whole marriage thing is over. I won't have my father's company anymore, but maybe I'll finally get to finish my fashion course in person, instead of from a computer screen. As long as I have the house, I don't really care. I would give up all my dreams of fashion designing if it meant holding on to this place.

But for now, I'm going to treat myself to a life of hedonistic fun and pleasure. Even living in that huge house of Zach's without having to worry about taking care of a thing is a great gift. I have grown to like Arnold. I'm not sure if he returns the sentiment, but he smiles a lot when he is around me so I'll take that as a yes. I still haven't had a chance to get my teeth into that amazing library, either, and I must give that a go when I get a...

My thoughts trail off when I spot a shop, just off the main high street area. A discreet sign announces it as an adult toy store. My heart does a loop-to-loop in my chest as I notice the window dressing. I bite my lip and glance around; no one is paying any attention to me, all of them too busy with their own business to care about a girl who is discovering her sexuality.

It's the kind of place I would have been embarrassed to be seen near in days gone by, but now...yeah, I have to admit, I'm curious. I go down the side street, open the door, and step into a world I have never ventured into before.

There are a few other people in there, but none of them pay me any attention which makes me feel bolder. No one looks ashamed or furtive so I take my time to look around the place. It is made up of more kinds of sex toys than I had even been aware existed.

Dildos and vibrators, sure, but so much more than that. Plugs with tapered ends and fur dangling off them, sleek pebble-shaped things that looked as though they would fit into the palm of my hand, objects with ears and attachments, whips, bunny tails, and so much more. I reach out and press the button on one of them, and it springs to life, buzzing loudly. I practically leap back.

One man looks up at me and smiles.

It is a smile of understanding, so I smile back.

I make my way around the store slowly, taking it all in. There's so much to see. From floggers, whips and paddles, to handcuffs, ropes and chains, outfits and toys...well, enough to keep me stocked for as long as I could imagine. My body is thrumming with excitement at the thought of him using some of the more interesting toys on me. I'm sure he'll know exactly what to do with them. I pick out a couple of things and head to the cashier.

As I am paying, my phone buzzes in my pocket. I finish the transaction before I answer it. My sister is calling. Probably to tell me what a great time she is having in the Porsche. I smile fondly as accept the call, but as soon as I hear her voice, my stomach drops.

"Scarlett?" she wails.

"Lori, what's wrong?"

"I crashed the car," she blurts out.

I can hear the fear in her voice, the panic, the doubt. And I know this is bad. "Are you okay?" I demand as I turn away from the counter.

She sniffles slightly. "I'm fine. Totally fine. I didn't get hurt at all."

"And the car?" I ask.

She falls silent for a moment.

Now, my shoulders sag.

"I'm so sorry!" she says with a sob. "I was just taking it out around a bend and I didn't see the other car coming."

I pinch the bridge of my nose. I can't believe this is happening. "How bad is the car?"

"Not good," she whispers.

"Where are you?"

"Just outside Wotton Hall."

"What are you doing there? Victoria doesn't want us there."

"I know. I know, but I just wanted to go visit Mom's grave. I just wanted to..." She begins to sob in earnest.

"I'm coming over there," I reply quickly as I stuff my latest purchases in my bag.

I need to take care of this before Zach finds out what happened, or I get the feeling that this little pre-honeymoon honeymoon period that we've been on is about to coming crashing to an abrupt halt.

CHAPTER 21

ZACH

I pace back and forth in my office, checking my phone over and over again. I still haven't heard from her. I've left what feels like a hundred messages and she still hasn't gotten back to me. My brain is in a state of full panic, and I feel like I am going to tip my desk over and tear up my own office if I don't get an answer as to what the fucking *hell* happened to Scarlett's car this afternoon.

Since the car is registered to me as the main driver, I got a call from the insurance company to let me know that the crash alarm had gone off just after lunchtime today.

"What are you talking about?" I demanded angrily, confused as to how this could be happening. Scarlett is a careful driver, careful in the way she is careful about everything that happens in her life. No way she could have let this go down.

"We received an alert that the car has suffered some major damage, Mr. Black," the woman on the other end of the line explained to me, clearly thrown by how harsh I sounded.

"And what happened?" I asked.

She hesitated. "I don't know..."

"Jesus Christ," I muttered, and hung up quickly.

And ever since then, I've been doing everything I can to get hold of Scarlett and figure out what the fuck happened. I need to know if she made it out all right. If I don't hear from her soon, I'm going to have to start calling hospitals.

I hear a small knock on the door. Only Scarlett knocks like that. I dash to the door and pull it open at once. On the other side is the woman that I have been waiting to hear from all day. She looks exhausted, but I am so worried about her that I pull her over the threshold and envelop her in a tight hug.

"Fuck, Scarlett, Where the fuck have you been?" I ask harshly.

She pulls away from me, glances around at Dahlia, then closes the door to make sure that she can't listen in on us.

"Are you all right?" I ask, my eyes roving over her body.

"I'm fine," she assures me. "My baby sister is, too."

I frown. "What?"

"Lori is the one who was driving the car when it crashed."

"Jesus, Scarlett. You let your little sister drive the car? She's not even insured," I fire angrily. I know I am just papering over the cracks of my worry with fury, but I can't stop myself. I don't want to.

"I'm sorry, I didn't think. She's a good driver," she explains quickly. "It was the other guy's fault. He didn't see her. The car's a wreck, but she's okay."

"Well, that's something," I mutter.

She furrows her brow at me. "How did you know about it, anyway?"

"The insurance company called me," I reply. "And that's why I've been trying to get hold of you all day. But you obviously didn't think this was important enough to warrant a call to put my mind at ease, huh?"

"I didn't even know you were worried—"

"And you thought I called you a hundred times just for the fun of it?" I snap.

She held her hands up defensively. "Hey, I was too busy taking care of my little sister to think about you." There is a barbed edge to her voice.

I can't believe she dares take that tone with me given what she put me through today. I move towards her.

She stares up at me boldly, not pulling her eyes from mine.

"Too busy to think about me?" I ask softly.

She bites her bottom lip and looks up at me defiantly.

"Well, fuck you too, Scarlett," I say, grabbing her hips.

Her breathing seems to stop. I love the power that I have over her in this regard, the way she bows to what I want, what I need from her, as though it is the most important thing in the world.

She stands on her tiptoes and kisses me, but I push her back against the door roughly, moving her hands above her head. She flexes her wrists against my hands and grinds her body into mine. *Fuck.* For a few hours this afternoon, I wasn't even sure I would ever get a chance to touch this body again.

I slip my hand beneath her top, running it over her belly, feeling the movement of her flesh beneath my skin. I'm never going to let her get in any danger, not as long as she is with me. I can't stand it. Then something about that emotion wells up into something else...I pluck her off the door and sit her down on my desk.

"What are you doing?" she pants.

I don't want to hear her speak. I rip off her panties. "Quiet now," I command. She opens her mouth to protest. Before she can say a word, I stuff the panties between her lips, quietening her for good. Her eyes widen, but she doesn't spit them out. I pull up her skirt, spread her legs roughly and push two fingers inside of her, I find that she is already wet and ready for my cock. The tension of everything that has happened today has morphed into something else, something dark and exciting.

"You want me to fuck you, Scarlett?" I growl in her ear, but she can't reply. I pull back to look at her.

With huge eyes, she nods at me, a flash of desperation in her gaze.

I reach into the drawer next to her and pull out a condom. Sheathing myself quickly I push her knees up so that I can expose her slick pussy. Pressing the head of my cock to her wet slit, I rub between her juicy lips, teasing her with it. "No time for me, huh?" I taunt.

She groans, and reaches out to pull me inside of her, but I push her hands away at once.

"Just because I'm crazy about this pussy doesn't mean you get to ignore me and think you call all the shots," I murmur, as I push myself inside of her. I love the look in her eyes when I take her like this, as her body gets used to the feeling of me filling her up. Like she is going crazy for my cock. I keep her hands pinned down by her sides and glide into her until I am buried inside her, all the way inside, just the way I like it.

See how it feels? See how much you want me?

I begin to pump into her, harder and harder, pushing in deep with every thrust, watching the way her eyes roll back as I take her, right here on the desk. The last time we did this, it was on her terms, but this time, it is on mine. And I don't want her to forget that.

"Don't come until I tell you to," I order.

She lets out a moan to tell me that she accepts the terms.

I thrust into her, really hard, the sound of our bodies clashing together fills the room, rubbing out all those images I'd had of her in some state of pain or broken. If anything had happened to her...I couldn't have handled it. I couldn't have handled her hurt. I needed her just like this, all mine, her body perfect, her legs open wide, her pussy full of *my* cock.

I sink my fingers into her hips and pull her towards me. I couldn't get deep enough inside her. It is like I want to wrap her up in me and never let her go. Everything that happened today has thrown into sharp relief just how much I want her. Just how much being with her has changed everything that I was sure I knew about myself. My breath tears out of my lungs as I move into her, driving myself deep.

I can feel her beginning to tense up, but she knows she has to wait for my command. Her thighs are beginning to clamp around me, drawing me in close, and her jaw is tight, but she is doing as I ordered. *Good girl.* I slow my movements, tormenting her with how close she must have been and yet how far I am from giving it to her.

"You want to come, Scarlett?" I ask her.

She nods, letting out another soft moan.

"Not yet," I breathe in her ear. I fuck her hard again, moving faster.

She groans and clasps on to the desk for dear life. She is rolling her hips back to meet mine, torn between wanting to give in and wanting to please me. But she holds out, choosing the latter, and I finally give her what she wants.

"Now," I order her, and as though I have flicked a switch, she comes. Hard. Her pussy convulsing crazily around my cock and her thighs clamping around me. Her eyes roll back into her head, and I kiss her neck, licking up her throat like I want to take a bite of it. This is how I want her. To be as helpless as she made me feel earlier today. Panties stuffed in her mouth so she can't make a sound, giving me what I want, when I want it.

Watching her climaxing like this pushes me over the edge. Intense pleasure shoots through me, and I let out a roar, not caring who hears me. Dahlia is outside, and probably knows just what is happening here. *Let her.* Maybe then, that'll teach her to back off, and she'll know I'm not interested in anyone but my Scarlett.

I pull the panties from her mouth and kiss her, deeply, our bodies still connected. Her hands brush up my back and cradle my head. I wrap my arms around her, forgetting for a moment that I am meant to be punishing her for leaving me hanging for so long without any word. I can't punish Scarlett. I'm just happy she's here, that she's fine.

Pulling out of her, I swiftly dispose of the condom. She puts her hand out for her panties, but I slip the wet material into my pocket.

She raises her eyebrows at me. "Haven't I been punished enough?"

"I think you enjoyed it a little too much for that, don't you?" I point out.

She grins. "So I have to go home without my underwear?"

"Exactly," I reply. "And I want you naked and waiting in bed for me when I get there."

"I should crash your cars more often," she remarks, cocking an eyebrow.

I clasp her face in my hands, looking intently into her eyes. "If something like this ever happens again, and you don't make it your priority to let me know what's happened, I won't play as nice," I tell her in a deadly serious tone.

Her eyes soften. "Didn't know you had it in you to be so concerned," she remarks.

I plant a kiss on her lips. I am just glad she is safe. Still a little mad that she made me wait so long to know that for sure, but I will take care of that tonight.

CHAPTER 22

SCARLETT

I lie in bed and stare at the ceiling. How can it be I am already starving for round two, when round one was a matter of hours ago?

Lori is safely back to her apartment in the city, not far from school. I think she is still reeling from the stiff telling-off I gave her for taking the car around the grounds in the first place. If Victoria caught her there, either of us there, she might use it in some way against us. Until Zach and I marry, we need to be super careful.

I am still surprised by how Zach reacted to the whole thing though. I was so nervous as I made it to his office. I saw all the missed calls and I was dreading telling him. I thought he would be mad about the car, but he didn't seem to give a damn about that. No, he definitely had no interest in the car. The way he held me, the way he took me, and even the way he came, roaring as if he didn't care that Dahlia would hear him. It had been something else entirely. I thought of his skin against mine, his breath on my neck, his roughness that felt like just a front to cover up his vulnerability.

I still don't know what to make of it.

But I do know that I'll have a good excuse to play with all the toys I purchased today to burn off all the adrenalin and tension from the last few hours still rushing around my system. And frankly, I can't think of a better way to do it.

I never thought in a million years that I would enjoy being controlled the way he controls me in bed. But when he tells me what to do, I feel...safe and protected. Like a child. No responsibilities. No fears. No worries. Nothing to do but have fun and enjoy myself. The outside world can hang back and wait, because I have my man here and he will guide me through what needs to be done, no matter what it might be.

Maybe that sounds crazy and a nightmare to a feminist, but it works for me.

I've spent too many years trying to control everything around me, trying to be the adult, the caregiver, the person who is strong, I finally have an excuse to let go and allow someone else to call the shots. And I'm sure as hell not going to say no to that, not when those shots are being called by one of the most gorgeous men I've ever seen in my life.

I hear the door open downstairs, and I shiver where I lay in bed. God, I'm so excited to see him. I went through the whole rest of my day without panties on, doing as he asked me to, and there was a thrill to knowing that I was honoring his commands when he wasn't even in the building with me.

Now, he is, and I can hear his footsteps mounting the stairs. A prince, a beast, I'm not sure what will walk through the door. I'm not sure if it matters. I close my eyes and bite my lip. I am so ready for this...

He opens the door, and I hear him inhale sharply when he sees me naked on the bed. Then his eyebrows rise when he spots the toys I have laid out for him. I picked out the ones that I thought looked the most exciting, selecting them carefully from the collection I had amassed earlier in afternoon, and I am pretty proud of the way I have taken the initiative.

"What are all these?" he asks quietly, as he makes his way over the bedside table. "Did you buy them?"

"Yes, I got them for us."

He glances over at me, a flash of amusement in his eyes. "I thought virgins were supposed to be innocent," he remarks, as he trails his fingers over the toys and bindings I've laid out for him to use.

"I was," I reply. "Until I met you..."

He plucks a butt-plug from the table, and tosses his blazer aside as he climbs on to the bed.

My heart begins to race. Just being this close to him is enough to get me going. I can already feel that keening, wailing need inside of me, and I am desperate for him to give it the attention it deserves.

"You ever used one of these before?" he asks.

I shake my head.

"Any reason you picked it out?" he continues, as he pushes my legs apart. I shake my head again, and he slides his hand beneath my ass, tugging me forward a few inches, so I am pressed right up against him. "You want me to show you how to use it?" he murmurs.

I nod, and a devious smile crosses over his face. I love it

when he looks at me like this. There is something so sexy about knowing that he wants to show me the ropes. Or whips, or chains, or butt-plugs...

He reaches over and grabs a bottle of lubricant from the bedside table. Even though there were dozens of different flavors, I decided that I just wanted the plainest one I could find. I need to start somewhere. Besides, as soon as he walks into the room, I become wet enough for him that he doesn't need to use anything like that... like I am now.

I watch as he applies a generous amount of lubricant to the plug, getting it good and slick. It is small, about the size of my thumb, but I've never had anything back there in my entire life and I'm not sure how I feel about the thought of it pushing into me. Excited, yes, but a little worried that it might hurt.

"Don't worry," he murmurs, as though he can sense the fact that I am a bit nervous. "Just trust me. If it gets too much for you, just tell me and we'll stop." He grabs my thighs and pushes them forward so my hips roll up off the bed, so that every part of me is completely exposed to him and he has easy access to all of it.

"Look how wet you are," he growls. And as if he can't resist, he bends his head and dips his tongue into my soaked pussy. I moan when he rolls his tongue in circular movements inside me. Raising his head, he then dips the plug into my pussy, covers it with my wetness, and then trails it down so slowly, I feel goosebumps scatter my skin.

"Ah!" I gasp as soon as I feel it pressing against my asshole. It is an odd feeling, not something I can compare to anything else. Good, I think? Hard to say because he is also stroking my hair and letting his hand trail down my naked body.

"Go with it," he murmurs, then he sucks my clit and presses the plug a little harder against me, twisting it around slightly, so that it slips a little inside of me.

I inhale sharply. It hurts a little, sure, but there is pleasure too from the sucking he is doing. The feeling mellows out into a lustful pleasure that runs from my tailbone to the nape of my neck. I shiver on the bed. He raises his head and I get my eyes to focus on him long enough to see the way he is looking at me. With complete and utter want. The power of his desire coaxes me to go a little further.

The plug slides into me further. Just another inch, but enough to make me moan. Okay, now I'm starting to get it. I can feel the sensation pulsing up between my legs to fill my pussy, the newness of it, the sheer novelty, enough to get me going.

"How does it feel?" he asks, as he makes little circles around my clit with his other hand.

My clit is pulsing and swollen, but all I can focus on is the new sensation inside me. "It feels...good, I think."

"You think?"

"I think I need more to know for sure," I say daringly.

He smiles wolfishly and pushes it a little further into me.

There's that shock again, that swiftly subsides into pleasure. There's a fullness to it that I've never felt before, and I like it, but I want more. I look into his eyes. "What else have you got?"

Still playing with my clit, he reaches over to the table, and plucks another toy from the collection. This time, a large, pink dildo with a couple of rabbit-ears on it meant to stimulate the clit.

My vision is starting to get a little blurry around the edges, the pleasure is turning out to be a lot to handle, but when I look at that thing, I know at once that I want it.

"You think you can handle this too?" he asks.

I feel as though he is daring me, but I have never been chicken when it comes to being challenged. "I can," I croak.

He pushes the plug deeper so that it will hold its place inside me, and reaches down to unzip his pants.

"I think I can give it to you," he agrees. "But I need to see if you can take this first..." And with that, he pulls his cock out of his pants and takes it into his hand.

I widen my eyes when I realize why he has arranged me in this position, what he is asking for.

He wants to fill every one of my orifices. He clicks the dildo on to vibrate, and lays it softly against my clit, rolling it back and forth. Then he moves his body and positions his cock near my mouth.

It looks so much bigger close-up.

"Think you can manage it?" he murmurs.

Yes! So, without another thought, I part my lips and take his cock into my mouth. As I take him into my mouth, he pushes the dildo into my pussy, and all at once, every single one of my holes has been filled at the same time.

To say that the sensation is overwhelming wouldn't even have come close to doing it justice. My brain feels like it is sizzling, trying to process every detail of the sensations radiating out of my orifices. The dildo feels big and hard, cold and foreign inside my pussy. My walls stretch to try and fit the whole thing inside of me. Because it is so hard it feels bigger than his cock and comes almost as a shock, but I breathe deep and try to get used to the way it feels inside of me.

But he is not finished. He pushes my knees further apart so that my bare breasts are exposed to him. With his cock in my mouth, I can't see what he is doing, so it is a shock when he fixes the nipple clamps on me.

The sensations are so new, so different, and so unfamiliar that my mind feels like it is being pulled in a hundred separate directions at once as I try to make sense of it all. I move my tongue over his cock as he pushes it all the way inside. He lets out a deep groan and that tells me I am doing something right.

I just let my instincts take over for me. I know that I can't fuck up too badly, since I have him in my mouth and he loves what I do to it. I feel a little flush work its way down my bare chest at the sheer effort this is taking from me.

But he is giving me all the time in the world I need to get used to it. Then, every time I fear that it might be getting too much and I'm going to have to let him down, he pushes the toys a little deeper inside of me, finding some new unchartered territory inside of me, and the pleasure that courses through me drives me to new heights.

I feel his cock ease in more and I worry that I am not going to be able to take him any deeper. Then, he twists the dildo around as the vibrating rabbit-ears press up against my clit, and I let out a groan. And just like that, his cock slides easily, further down my throat, taking me by surprise.

The gag reflex I have been fighting with ever since I started giving him blow jobs falls away and I feel wild for him. Every one of my holes is being penetrated, and I can't get enough. He begins to move his hips slightly, guiding himself deeper into my throat. I slide my hands around his firm buttocks and get a good hold on him.

I am surprised by how ravenous I feel for his cock. I wish I could take him even deeper, wish that he would fuck my mouth the way he is fucking my pussy with the dildo, but I know that I'm probably not ready for that yet. It's better for us to take our time and build up to things slowly, than to push too far too fast.

I moan around his cock as I feel myself getting close.

God, it feels so good to have him between my legs, thrusting that dildo deep inside of me like he's imagining it's his own cock. I am getting closer and closer, so close I can hardly take it. I am teetering on the very brink, ready to give in, to give out, to let this take me past the abyss.

I want to hold and wait for him to direct me, but my body crests. The orgasm hits me hard without warning. My cries are gagged by his cock in my mouth, but I know he must be able to feel them running up and through his body. My pussy clenches hard around the plastic inside of me, my ass tightening around the plug, and it feels like the pleasure is pouring into me from all angles.

I can hardly make sense of it—it's so much, all at once.

He pulls his cock from my mouth and pumps it a few times, and before I know it, he has covered my chest with his warm cum.

I gasp and catch my breath, the warmth of it trickling over my skin – and I am surprised by how much I like it. He has marked me as his. As though I didn't know it already. Reaching for his hips, I pull his cock back into my mouth and suck the last remaining cum dripping from it.

"Fuck, Scarlett," he gasps.

My whole body is shivering with the intensity of what has just happened and all I can do is lie there, even though I know I should take the toys out and go clean myself up.

Gently, he disengages his cock from my mouth.

"Did I do good?" I ask.

He moves to lay beside me on the bed and kisses me, almost ferocious in his intent, then presses his forehead to mine. "Yes, baby," he assures me, and it's the first time he has ever used such a pet-name for me. "You did good."

I reach down to take the toys from inside me, but he stops me.

"Leave them," he says. "I'm not finished with you."

CHAPTER 23

I t's our wedding day today. Our marriage is supposed to be a sham and everything about it is a lie, but it doesn't feel that way to me.

We threw this wedding together in no time. Hell, I'm not even sure that it earns the title of a wedding, really. We only have two guests, Molly, Scarlett's friend and Lori, her little sister. And even they are just here to fulfill their roles as the emotional support for Scarlett. I didn't want to involve my family. They'd know something is not right. They'd know I would never get married in a place like this. But in truth, they wouldn't believe I would marry anyone, anywhere.

Scarlett told me she won't even be wearing white. Shame, because if any woman deserved to wear white it was her. Although she wouldn't show me what she had picked out to wear, I'm still looking forward to seeing her come down the aisle, even if the place is almost empty and she's running five minutes late.

"Do you want me to check on her?" The woman tasked with conducting the civil ceremony asks.

"No need. She'll be here," I reply confidently. I know she will be. I can trust her.

And that's the real problem. I've never met a woman I could say that about. She fits the bill in every way possible. So why is this marriage a sham?

It would have been easy if I had just been able to brush this marriage off as what it was: the two of us doing what we had to in order to get what we needed from the arrangement. But I can't do that anymore.

Now, I look forward to coming home at the end of a long day and seeing her. She always makes sure she's there for me when I arrive back, and her face lights up when she looks up from her book and meets my gaze.

And the sex.

Christ, the sex has to be some of the best I've ever had in my life, and it's not like I haven't had a lot of it. I thought being with a virgin would lose its charm pretty quickly. I mean, who remains a virgin until they are twenty years old? Only an uptight prude, that's who. But Scarlett is wild and uninhibited and ready to try new stuff all the time.

Her curiosity is boundless. I never know what I am coming home to. There's so much she wants to try, as though she's catching up on all this stuff, and I am more than happy to make sure that she does.

I hear the rustling of fabric. I turn around to see Molly and Lori, her best friend and her sister. My gaze swings past them and I know that my face lights up with a smile of pure happiness when I see Scarlett coming towards me.

She is wearing a cream suit, cut close to her body. It suits her perfectly. Not just the way it looks, but the way it hugs her curves. There are flowers in her hair. Somehow, that makes me a little sad. This isn't the way it should be for her. She should have the whole nine yards. The wedding planner, the guests, the church wedding, the confetti, the professional photographer. This is bullshit. I swear right then that one day, I'll make it better.

She joins me, and I take her hand.

She smiles up at me, and her eyes are a little misty.

I wonder if I have the same look on my face. I'm not sure where the line between reality and myth exists anymore. Because to me, this is a real wedding.

"Are we ready to begin?" The officiant asks.

I can't speak, so I nod.

Now, the ceremony starts.

A few weeks ago, I would have been rushing to get through this, checking my watch to see if I had time to head down to a meeting afterwards, or make a conference call with some of my employees across the country. But time seems to fall away as I stand here, going through the ceremony with Scarlett Johnson at my side. She said she wouldn't take my name. Too much hassle, she claimed, given that we aren't even really going to be together. But even so, some part of me wants her to carry my name. It suits her. Scarlett Black. What a wonderful name it is. Good enough to be a stage name.

The woman asks the obligatory question if anybody present has any objections, to state them now or be forever silent.

Her friend Molly pretends to raise her hand, then pulls her own raised hand down with her other hand.

Lori giggles.

Scarlett shakes her head, but she is smiling.

The woman conducting the ceremony frowns and carries on.

"I do," Scarlett murmurs.

Her eyes look so soft and beautiful I think I will remember this moment forever. I lean in to kiss her. It is the first time we have kissed in front of anyone else, and it feels odd. I know that this is for show. I also know that Lori and Molly realize that it's for show, but it feels real. And guess what? I wish it were real.

I slip the ring onto her finger and just like that... she becomes my wife.

The officiant closes her book and seems to relax a little, letting go of some of the tension she had been radiating. She chats to us a little as we make our way out and confesses this was the first marriage she has performed.

Scarlett laughs and tells her she did really well as she takes my hand. I can feel her ring against my skin and it feels...good. Which surprises me, because I'd always envisioned these metal bands as little shackles meant to bind the wearer. With her, it's different. It's special. It's a small loop that contains everything we have shared together within it.

"So, where are you guys going on your honeymoon?" The officiant asks.

I haven't even thought about that, and I know we're going to be too busy putting her plan into action to think about travelling anywhere.

But irrepressible Scarlett is there to step in. "Thailand," she replies, and she looks at me with a smile. "We both love the food and well, my husband loves it, but he's never taken me there before and we thought it would be the most beautiful place to kick things off between us."

"Oh, that sounds wonderful," the woman remarks.

I notice Molly raising her eyebrows next to us. She knows that it's all made up, but she at least has the sense to keep her mouth shut about it.

"Yes, it really does," I reply, but in my head, I only hear the words *my husband* from her lips. And it sounds good. Real good.

As soon as we are alone again and headed back to the apartment, I turn to her. "How did you come up with Thailand so quickly?"

"Because I've thought about it before," she admits. "I mean, not with you. But I always thought that when I do get married, I'd want to honeymoon in Thailand. I love Thai food and it's gorgeous there, so much history..." She smiles dreamily.

I simply stare the way the sunshine slants in through the window and frames her face and it is enough to take my breath away. There is only one way I know of for how to deal with all the crazy emotions running through my body.

I take her home and fuck us both senseless.

When I wake up next to her in the morning, the hardest thing in the world is to convince myself to get out of bed and leave her. I wish I could find some excuse to have her come into the office with me. She clings to me and I wonder if the same thing is going through her mind, but she says nothing.

When I head in to work, my mind is so full of her that it feels like there is no room for anything else. Even as I close the door, I already miss her so much it feels like my whole body is crying out for her. She feels like an addiction that I cannot stave off.

Scarlett is the only thing on my mind, as I open the door to my office, and my jaw drops.

CHAPTER 24

SCARLETT

I walk along the sunlit corridor towards his office while admiring the glint of my wedding ring in the light. It's strange, seeing it out of the corner of my eye, but I like the way it looks. It suits me, I think. It's simple and plain, but I know he probably spent a bomb on it, given that his solution to everything is always to just to pay more for the best he can get.

I can't believe I'm doing this. As soon as he left home, I missed him so much I had to see him. Maybe he will throw me out and tell me that office hours are sacred, but I don't care. I have to see him.

He left some files on his desk this morning so I decided I'd do the good-wifely thing and bring them in for him. Arnold offered to go for me, but of course, I insisted on taking myself up to the office. I told him I wanted to hang on to a little of my independence. It's so easy, in that flawlessly run mansion to forget I ever had to do anything for myself, but of course, the real reason was completely selfish. I missed Zach like mad.

I promised myself I wouldn't make a nuisance of myself. It'll be a fleeting visit only, then I'll drop in on Lori, to make sure that she's not throwing wild house parties all the time. Not that I imagine her as the kind of teen who would do that, but still... I hadn't imagined she would crash my car, either and yet, she did.

As I rush down the corridor, I remember the way I felt when he saw me coming down the aisle towards him, that smile spreading out over his face as though he couldn't believe how lucky he was. Maybe he is just a really good actor, but for a moment, I actually believed it.

However, when I said fleeting visit, I meant long enough to fuck his brains out.

My mind is already racing at the thought of what we could do while I'm up in his office. After all, he can barely keep his hands off me when we are alone together. I've never felt more wanted, or desired in my life.

What he said when we first got together is branded in my psyche, that he would move on as soon as he got bored, but so far, he certainly didn't seem bored. Though I couldn't help but worry about the way he might sneak around behind my back, keeping me as an easy lay, back home while he could...I push open his door and come to abrupt halt. I swear to God, I freeze on the spot.

There is a woman inside, a woman I recognize at once. Dahlia.

She is splayed out on his desk, in nothing but a jacket, which is open to show off her slim, toned naked body. I can't believe this is happening. Zach is standing over her. They both don't seem to notice me, and I hang back more of shock than anything else. Maybe he has been having an affair with her the whole time? Maybe that's why she was so pissed whenever I slipped into his office for a cheeky hook-up before?

"Come on, Zach," Dahlia coos, her voice dripping with honey. "You're really telling me that you don't want all this?"

"I really am," he snarls back.

My heart leaps. He doesn't know I'm here. There's no reason for him to tell her he doesn't want her or for her to be asking him if he doesn't want her, if they really are involved. Which means that she must just be trying to seduce him, even though the bitch knows he's married to me now.

The relief in my gut twists up and into something else entirely, white-hot fury blasts into my head. If Dahlia thinks she can just slither in here and try to hook up with my husband, then she has another 'thing' coming.

I make a noise.

As soon as Dahlia sees me, she pulls her coat shut and leaps to her feet. "Scarlett," she coos, like she could really convince me that she's nothing but sweetness and light right now.

"Scarlett, listen to me—" Zach tells me urgently.

I lift my hand to silence him, though I never take my narrowed eyes off Dahlia. "You need to get out of here, slut," I tell her.

She raises her eyebrows at me and rises to her feet.

I can't believe the gall of the woman. It's like she's delusional, genuinely of the belief that this is how things are meant to roll, that she is the one in the right here.

"Scarlett, you just need to accept the fact that the man you married has needs outside of your relationship," Dahlia tells me, her voice laced with a patronizing edge. "Needs that you can't fulfil. Needs that I can."

Her condescending tone makes my stomach clench.

"He's *never* had anything to do with you. You couldn't satisfy him if you laid on your back and shot ping pong balls out of your vagina," I shoot back. Zach told me before, he doesn't do this, not with people he works with and I believe him. He may be many things, but he is not a liar. Not to mention the fact, well, I don't think she's really his type. I've seen the way he looks at my body, the way he touches me like he can't get enough, and I doubt skinny assed Dahlia would do a lot for him.

"We're together," Dahlia tells me confidently, tossing her hair over her shoulder. "He's just playing right now because he knows he's been busted."

I look to Zach.

Silent, he is looking at me with an expression of almost awe. Not at all the look of a guilty man.

I don't want to hear another word out of her mouth. I turn back to her. "Get out of here. You're fired."

"Zach needs me. I'm the only one who knows how everything works!" Dahlia responds, but she looks a little panicked. Finally, it seems like the reality of the situation is setting in. Her face has gone pale and her eyes are wide.

I want her worried. I want her upset. I want her to know what happens when someone tries to come after *my* husband.

"You don't have the power to do that," she flings at me.

I am surprised by the fire in my belly, the heat pulsing through my system, but it's there, and I'm going to be damned if I let some random woman who thinks that she's got a chance in hell to get close to my man. Before I can open my mouth, Zach cuts in.

"No, but I do. And I want you gone. Out of here. Clear your desk by the end of the day and I'll make sure you get your two months severance pay."

She glares at him furiously before sweeping out of the office and slamming the door so hard behind her the window shakes.

I exhale and turn to Zach. "Please, tell me that nothing was going on between you two?" I beg. "Please tell me I didn't just make an ass of myself for nothing."

Zach looks into my eyes.

I can see it there in his gaze and I know the truth.

CHAPTER 25

ZACH

"**N**othing was going on between us," I tell her, and I mean it. I know I can't convince anyone of the truth just like that, but judging by the way she reacted, I don't think she's going to need a lot of convincing.

Scarlett exhales a long breath and claps her hand to her chest. "Thank fucking Christ, because if I've just fired a woman over nothing..."

"You haven't," I assure her, walking towards her and clasping her arms. "Nothing has ever happened between the two of us, and it never would have. If you hadn't fired her, I would have. At the very least, she would have been transferred to another department."

"Yeah, I know that," she admits and smiles at me.

And my whole body lights up when I see that soft look on her face.

"I heard you brushing her off before I made a noise," she continues. "But for a wild second, I thought—I thought maybe it was for show, not because you were actually trying to get rid of her..."

"You believed me," I murmur.

She furrows her brow at me. "What?"

"You believed me," I repeat. "You have no idea...I can't think of anyone else who would have believed me in that situation. Especially, with the reputation I have. I think that was what Dahlia was counting on."

"I knew you wouldn't do that to me," she says.

I take her face in my hands and look intently into her eyes. "Nobody has ever just believed me before," I tell her.

Her loyalty shines bright in her face, her trust in me warms my heart as a secure feeling settles over me.

Scarlett reaches up and kisses me softly, on the mouth, as if sealing the precious moment between us.

And I know that it is sacred, because a bond of trust has been solidified, one that I would never have believed was there before. She actually took my word, took my side, without a second thought. When it comes to my reputation, I'm used to people brushing me off in favor of what they've heard about me, for the juicier story. But she didn't do that. She gave me the benefit of the doubt. And she is right, I would never betray her like that. Ever.

I wrap my arms around her and pull her in close against my body. The two of us stand here joined as one. It's the first time since we got together that I've really understood what it means to be a part of a partnership with her. To have her trust, her loyalty, her sureness, her confidence in me.

She loops her arms around my shoulders and I kiss her deeply. Everything that happened before she came is already falling from my mind. It seems useless now, hazy, like it might have happened to someone else entirely.

"Zack, have you ever wanted to go into me bare?"

I stare at her in astonishment. "Yes, but—"

"I'm on the pill now, so we're good to go."

"Damn, Scarlett. I would like nothing better than to feel your pussy on my cock."

"Well, what are you waiting for then?" she asks cheekily.

I bury my face in her neck then slide my hand up and under her shirt, tracing my fingers over the lace of her bra. She moans softly as I guide her back towards the chair behind us. I want to see her while I take her, look into her eyes while I make her mine again.

She climbs on top of me, knowing at once, what I want from her, and rolls her skirt up to reveal herself to me. Her body is so perfect, every curve drawn in beauty. I can't help comparing her to Dahlia and finding Dahlia a dull shadow in comparison. She slides her panties down over her hips and tosses them aside.

I pull myself free of my pants, taking my cock into my hand.

She grips the back of the chair for leverage. "Zach, I..." she murmurs, but before the words can come out of her mouth, I kiss her again.

I feel like I know what she is going to say, anyway, and honestly, the thought of hearing her speak it out loud feels far too dangerous for my liking. I slide one hand over her hip and

RIVER LAURENT

guide her down on top of me, so that she is impaled on my thick cock. The sensation is wonderful. Not since I was a reckless teenager, have I gone bareback and it felt nothing like this. In fact, I have been with so many women before but not one of them has come close to making me feel the way she does.

I thrust up into her, pushing myself deep, so I can feel her all the way around my cock. Her pussy is wet, warm and welcoming, slick and tight around me, and she gasps with pleasure as I take her for the first time skin-on-skin. I am always surprised by how well the two of us fit together, how well we seem to make sense, but bare—we are incredible. I feel powerful when I'm with her, and vulnerable at the same time.

She grasps the back of the chair and slides her hips from side to side, testing out the way this new position feels to her.

I gaze up at her and just take her in.

This is my wife.

My wife.

I love watching my wife exploring new positions. She goes completely on instinct, purely on what feels good to her in the moment, and who am I to deny that? This isn't a performance for my benefit, she's just doing what makes her feel good, and all I want to do is sit back and let her find her sweet spots.

I move my hands to her hips and feel them rise and fall on top of me. I go slow at first, moving gently, and then a little harder, till I am driving myself deep into her with every thrust.

She moans, and then moans again, louder.

She can yell for all I care, as there is no one outside to catch us in the act or overhear us. Not that I would have cared much even if there were. The look on her face is everything I need and nothing else in the world matters to me at this moment.

"Fuck," she gasps, as she turns her mouth to mine and kisses me roughly, her tongue finding my own at once. She has grown so much bolder, far removed from the nervous, curious version of herself from the very first time we fucked. I can't wait to see how she will grow and change as her sexuality matures, and she discovers sides to herself she never knew existed.

I push her hips down on my cock, harder this time, feeling my full length inside of her now. The thought of filling her with my seed for the first time fills me with wild excitement. I want to shoot it as deep into her body as possible, then I want to shut her legs and keep it inside her. A strange thought occurs to me. I wish she wasn't on contraceptives. I wish my seed would grow inside her.

"Ah!" she cries out.

Instantly, I feel her contract around my cock. I move deep inside her and hold myself there, letting her milk me with her pulsing pussy as she comes. Her body begins to tremble, and she shivers as she pushes herself down on top of me one more time. Like she is wringing the last drops of pleasure that she can from this moment.

I wrap my arms around her and rock slowly inside of her until I reach my own release, and shoot my cum deep inside her. It feels amazing and it takes some time to come down from my high.

Gently, I kiss a bare strip of shoulder that has been exposed by our fucking. I love her skin, so milky, soft and creamy. In the mornings, when I'm awake before her, sometimes I will just lie there to admire the way the sun glints here and there along her skin, making it glow while she is sleeping. Not that I would ever admit that to her, of course.

Scarlett slowly lifts herself off of me and slides instead into my lap. She leans her head against my shoulder, and then slips her hand over my chest, placing it on my heart. "Your heartbeat is so fast." She giggles. "Was it that good?"

I turn, and plant a kiss against her head. Being this close to her, I know that my heart isn't going to slow down any time soon.

"It was better than that good," I murmur into her sweet smelling hair.

CHAPTER 26

SCARLETT

One month later

"I can't believe this is happening," I tell Lori excitedly, as I check my hair for the thousandth time since I came through the door to her apartment. "Do I look all right?"

"He's speaking to you about fashion, not about becoming a hairstylist," Lori reminds me, lightly teasing.

Despite her teasing, I know she is excited for me. I step back and look at my outfit again. "I'm meant to take one thing off before I go out, right?" I remark. "That's the rule for fashion stuff..."

"I think you look perfect," she assures me as she gets to her feet and straightens the blazer that I am wearing.

"You sure?" I ask fretfully. I'm just worried. So much is hanging on this, and I can't believe that this is even happening in the first place. It doesn't make sense. But for once, things have just turned out well for me. Maybe I should embrace that. To embrace the fact that it's finally time for things to start working out for me.

When I got the call from Mark Simpson's personal secretary the week before, I'd been sure that it was some kind of joke. I am still not sure that it isn't, come to think of it. I keep waiting for the rug to be pulled out from beneath me while I look like a fool for believing it.

Anyway, when the call came, I assumed it was someone from the estate calling to discuss the details of my inheritance since I didn't recognize the number.

"Hi, is this Mrs. Scarlett Black?" a woman asked.

"Yes," I admitted cautiously. No one called me Scarlett Black.

"Good. I'm glad we finally got hold of you," she continued warmly. "I'm calling on behalf of Evangelion Outfitters. We would like to arrange a meeting with you at some point in the next couple of weeks to discuss a potential collaboration?"

A collaboration? With me?

I couldn't say a word. There was no way this was real. Evangelion Outfitters were one of the biggest fashion houses in the city. I had put in an application to take on an internship there at some point last year, but nothing had come of it. I was disappointed since I assumed it had gone to some more qualified candidate. The only other person who knew about my application was Molly. I waited for her to snatch the phone from one of her friends and laugh at me for believing the joke. But she didn't. Instead, the woman waited patiently for me to respond.

"Ah…a collaboration? Can you explain please?" I blurted out finally.

"Mark Simpson, the head of design, saw your wedding pictures," she explained.

There were paparazzi outside who snapped a few photos of us, and I supposed they must have made it out to some gossip blog or another, but I had never expected to hear anything of them again. But I always forget: Zach's life is of interest to other people, the way mine alone has never been.

"And we realized we had an application of yours on file," she continued. "So we looked at it again and he just loved the designs in your Lookbook. If you are not with any other fashion house yet, then you must come and meet us."

My jaw dropped. It's the last thing I expected to come out of this. The Lookbook I sent them was a class project. My teacher thought it was great, but I had never thought, not in a million years, that a real designer would look at it and see some potential in me. Especially, not a house as big as Evangelion Outfitters.

"No, no, I'm with no other fashion house," I almost screamed. "Yes, of course, I'd love to come and meet Mark Simpson! Where do you want to meet? And when? I'm pretty free and easy…" At that point, I forced myself to stop blurting out anymore insane comments and just waited for her to find a date that was convenient. When I hung up, I did a little dance of joy.

I couldn't believe I had a meeting with the kind of company who, as my father would very colorfully say, wouldn't even have pissed in my ear if I was on fire, only a few months before. It was a little disconcerting, of course, to know that my connection with Zach was what got me there. But hey, they would never have had my application if I hadn't taken the initiative and filled out that form myself. I've never looked a gift horse in the mouth and I'm not going to start now.

So here I am, just an hour or so away from the meeting, and no one has pointed to the hidden cameras to remind me what a fool I am.

"Quit fretting. You look amazing. What time is Zach coming?" Lori asks.

Zach is coming by Lori's apartment to pick me up and take me to the meeting. I told him he didn't need to come, but he wanted to. "I think it's cool as hell and I want to be the one who takes you to your big break," he told me firmly.

"Nothing to do with the fact that I'm going to be going out to lunch with another man all by myself, now, is it?" I asked playfully.

He wound his arms around my waist. "Nothing at all. I don't trust men, but I trust you," he murmured, and he kissed me.

I told him he honestly might be the perfect man and he laughed, but I have to say, since that episode with Dahlia, our relationship has only grown stronger by the day. I hadn't realized how much I could trust him until I had heard him brushing her off like she meant nothing to him.

"You're going to do great, I know it," Lori tells me, and gives me a quick hug. "I'm so proud of you, you know."

"Thank you," I reply, and squeeze her back. She is the only family I have left now and I feel extremely protective of her.

"You're keeping up with your studies and everything, aren't you?" I fret.

She rolls her eyes. "Oh, don't start."

"I know I am just being the overprotective big sister, but that's my job and I'm not letting it slide just because I'm not living with you anymore."

"Okay, okay. I'm keeping up with my studies just fine, all right?" she says with a laugh. "You have nothing to worry about, really. Just go and enjoy this lunch. You're going to nail it."

"I just want to make sure everything is all right with you."

She smiles sadly. "You're not Mom, remember?"

Hearing those words out of her mouth makes me fall silent for a moment. She's right, I'm not our Mom, but I could be someone's mom soon. My period is a bit late. Since I'm on the pill, I haven't panicked yet, or even picked up a test. I'll wait a few more days. The doctor did say things could be a bit wobbly to start with.

Before I can linger anymore on that thought, the doorbell rings.

Lori runs to opens it.

CHAPTER 27

SCARLETT

Zach is standing there waiting for me. He greets his sister-in-law with a smile. "You're enjoying having a bachelorette pad all to yourself?"

She grins at him. "I'd like it more if I could live in a mansion like you."

"Lori," I gasp.

Zach laughs and holds his hands up as if conceding defeat. He turns to me, still shaking his head at her teasing. "You look great," he says enthusiastically, as he checks out my outfit.

"Thank you," I murmur. It's really a redo of my wedding look but in darker colors. I think it looks cool, but I'm not sure if it's truly a good fit for the Evangelion Outfitters's brand.

"Ready to go?" he asks.

I nod. Then I give Lori a quick hug goodbye before I take his arm and let him lead me out of my sister's apartment. My heart is pounding in my chest. I can't believe I am going to meet with Mark Simpson of Evangelion Outfitters. Actually, from the day I went to see Zach in his office and asked him to marry me, I can't believe any of what has been happening to me.

Zach drives me across town.

I watch the people on the street going about their business. At this time, Zack is usually hard at work. While being married to him, I've learned a lot about him. How he started from almost nothing. How hard he works. How important his work is to him. "Why did you really want to come with me today?" I ask him.

He glances over at me and sighs, clearly deciding whether or not he's actually going to tell me the truth. "Look, I've been to these kinds of things before," he explains finally. "With guys like him. And trust me, from my experience, they use their power in these situations to...to get what they want."

"What do you mean?"

"He's just contacted you out of the blue, pretty much, right?"

"Well, I did send an application."

"Yeah, last year. He doesn't know much about you, other than the fact that you haven't got an established brand in the industry yet."

"So?" I press, furrowing my brow.

"So he knows that he might be able to use that."

"Use that?" I echo.

"Yes, use that. Don't fool yourself. Every industry has its casting couch, Scarlett."

"But he knows I'm married to you—"

"That never stops them, trust me," he replies. "In fact, sometimes I think it encourages them. Taking what belongs to another man is exciting for them."

I fall silent as he pulls the car to a halt.

He notices how quiet and withdrawn I have become, and he reaches over to take my hand. "I don't mean to freak you out. Chances are, he's going to be just fine, but I wouldn't be doing my job if I didn't look out for you when it comes to stuff like this. I'm a man, so I understand other men."

"All right," I mutter. I am a little thrown by what he has just told me, but I suppose he has a point. The chances of this being all purely innocent are not zero, but I hope and pray it's so.

"You ready to go in?" Zach asks.

I nod.

"Okay, let's do this." He nods at me.

I get out of the car, then Zach and I head into the restaurant together. It is the kind of fancy, upscale place that my father would have loved. He never threw his cash around, but when it came to celebrating big events, he always loved to book tables in lavish restaurants like this one, for the whole family.

I can still remember Lori sipping on champagne and giggling at the gathering, he held to celebrate my last birthday. I smile fondly at the memory, and some of the tension I'd been carrying leaves my body. Okay, I can do this. I can make this work. I know it might be hard, but if my father could spend so much of his life coming from the ground up to pull his life together, then I could do the same thing.

"Scarlett!" A voice calls to me, and I turn to see Mark Simpson sitting at a table against the wall. His eyes slide over to Zach at once, and his jaw tightens for a split second.

I see it but I ignore it. I don't want to believe Zach might be right.

Then he smiles and comes towards me to kiss me on both cheeks. He smells of expensive, slightly overwhelming after-shave. He is dressed in a pink shirt and a pair of slacks that were probably hand-crafted for him specifically.

"This is my husband, Zach," I introduce Zach to Mark.

The two men shake hands and give each other a hard look.

This is just how businessmen are with one another though, right? Nothing to read into, just the two of them trying to prove their respective dominance in this field. I take a seat, and the waiter immediately approaches with a bottle of wine.

"I think I'm okay," I turn it down politely, but Mark tells him to go ahead and pour because it is a celebration. I turn to Mark and raise my eyebrows, but he lifts his glass and touches it against mine.

"I thought it was only right that we celebrate this union," he remarks, as his eyes linger on mine just a little too long.

I brush it off. I'm reading into things because of what Zach said to me in the car. There's nothing here. There's no way that someone like Mark Simpson is going for me when he could have any woman in the city he wanted.

"Well, yes, I suppose our marriage wasn't that long ago," I say, deliberately misunderstanding him. I take a sip of the wine to show I'm game, even though this is meant to be a business meeting and I don't want to get tipsy.

"I was talking about you and I," Mark replies.

My eyes widen with shock. Is Zach right about him? He is acting as though Zach isn't even here.

"I took a look over your application, Scarlett, and we'd love to take you on board at Evangelion."

I stare at him in disbelief. Wow! How wrong has Zach been? I thought this was just going to be a chance for us to get to know each other, for him to parse out how much I actually knew about fashion before he thought about offering me a place. "Are you serious?" I squeal, when I find my voice.

I notice a few people glancing around from their tables, but I don't care. I've dreamed of hearing those words from an executive of a fashion house for so long. And now, here I am, sitting with my husband and the man who's at the forefront of fashion in this city while he is telling me his company wants me to be part of it.

He finishes his wine and nods. "I was very impressed by the sketches you sent in as part of your application. And your wedding outfit, and I thought it was so wonderfully classic. Almost breakfast at Tiffany-ish."

Zach holds my hand under the table.

I glance at him and beam. My expression telling him, see you were wrong. Everything is okay. After that, Mark and I spend the rest of the lunch talking fashion, stylists, models and designers. It feels so surreal, to be sitting here opposite him, to have him actually give a damn about my opinions, to listen to me and hear me out. He seems genuinely curious as to what I have to say, and I can't help being flattered.

"Obviously, I'd want to work closely with you at first," Mark tells me, as we wait for the bill to arrive. "You're so new, I wouldn't want to throw you out there by yourself right away..."

"I'm sure I could cope," I assure him. "You don't need to worry about me, really."

"There's nothing wrong with a little friendly lookout," Mark points out.

Zach's grip tightens on my hand beneath the table.

The lunch finishes with Mark giving me his number and landing another two kisses on my cheek. I guess the fashion world is a very expressive place. I head back out to the car feeling a little giddy with excitement.

"Can you believe it?" I say, feeling as though my head is going to pop with the enormity of everything.

"This is huge for you and I'm really proud of you," Zach says with a smile. He is trying to be pleased for me, but I know there is something nagging at the back of his brain. I furrow my brow at him. "What is it?"

"It's nothing," he says as he opens the car door for me.

I climb into the car, but I don't allow him to close the door. "It's not nothing. Tell me what it is."

"Okay. There's something off about that guy. I don't know what, but there's something not *right* about the way he operates."

"I think you're just looking for problems where there aren't any," I tell him, but I am feeling a prickle of uncertainty even as the words come out of my mouth. I want to believe what I'm saying, because the alternative would be...well, the most disappointing thing that I can think of.

Zach seems so sure, I don't want to dismiss it out of hand.

After all, Mark did seem overly enthusiastic about me, given that my only experience in the industry was an online course and a few sketches that I hadn't even had time to turn into garments yet.

"Time will tell," Zach says cryptically.

Yes, time will tell. I truly hope Zach is wrong. I lean back in the car seat, watching the workers walking along the sidewalks outside. I think excitedly about the fact that soon enough, I'm going to be one of them.

CHAPTER 28

ZACH

"**A**re you ready to sign the contracts on the Bilson holdings, Sir?"

I look up from my desk and at my new PA. Nathan, a slightly jittery twenty-eight-year-old who I'm pretty sure has no designs of splaying out naked on my desk in front of me. Shit, even the thought of what Dahlia did still makes me cringe. I couldn't imagine wanting to be with someone less than when I saw her without her clothes. She really thought she was God's own gift to me.

"Yes, sure, just bring them in," I reply.

After a few minutes, he returns to the office with a cluster of papers. He hands them over to me.

I take a look over the next company carcass I'll be picking through. Bilson Holdings, a real estate company with a vast network of agencies in the suburbs, is in the beginning stages of rot. There just isn't enough interest in their overpriced, under-marketed houses to keep them afloat in these lean times so I have been circling them for a while, keen to get them before the other vultures circling swoop in.

The contracts are all ready for me to sign. I scan through them and pick up my pen to fill out the appropriate part of the form and sign it, but I find myself hesitating. I put the pen down and swivel around to face the window.

Why am I hesitating? What's on my mind?

I know it is a sure thing. I've done this before. So what's going on with me? This company has been in the Bilson family for generations. The company probably isn't far removed from the kind of business that Scarlett inherited from her father.

But recently, it was passed down to the youngest son, who's only twenty-five. He has a fluff college degree and chances are he hasn't been raised to get his head around the level of skill and prestige it takes to convince people to buy homes or getting any real training. In business, any weakness means death. It's the law of the concrete jungle. I'd expect the same to happen to my company if I was stupid enough to leave it in the care of a naïve kid.

But these people are probably decent.

Building a real estate business in that side of town could never have been easy, so there had to be some business acumen in the family. Maybe with a little help, they could actually turn their company around. It might sound crazy, even to my own ears, but did I really need to break up their company just to make a profit? There is more than one way to skin a cat. Maybe I can try something different. Maybe I can approach it with something else in mind.

I grab the phone, checking the number on the contracts, and dial it up quickly, before I have a chance to talk myself out of this course of action.

A few moments later, an exhausted man's voice comes down the line, "Hello?"

"Hello, is this Tom Bilson?" I ask.

"Yes, that's me," he replies. He sounds confused and so young.

I was that young once.

"How did you get this number? It's not on any of our bill-boards anymore."

"I need to talk to you about your business."

He snorts with incredulity.

I can tell that he is already tired out by the very thought of this conversation.

"What business?"

"My name is Zachary Black," I say. "And I think I can help you there..."

I pinch the bridge of my nose and wince. Am I really doing this? Is this who I am now? A voice in my head goes, yes, and I launch into my spiel. I explain to him how he might be able to save his business. It surprises me how easily the words fall off my tongue, given it's against my natural instincts, or my best interest. I could have got my hands on some prime real estate if I just let his company fail, and yet, there is some-thing in me, telling me to try and help. Where no one else would.

"I just don't know if we have the capital to start turning

things around," he admits. "Don't get me wrong, if we had had this a few months ago, maybe even a year, it would have been different, but now…"

"I'll put up the capital," I reply at once. Like I said, there are more ways than one to skin a cat.

He becomes utterly silent.

I can hear the static of his sharp exhale over the line. He can't believe what I am offering him.

"You mean that?"

"Yes," I reply. "I'll put up half-a-million, and you can start rebranding and rebuilding from there, but you'll have to keep me in the loop, so I know the money is being put to good use."

"Yeah, of course we can," he replies at once, then he hesitates again. "Can I ask you something? And trust me, I've heard all that stuff about looking a gift horse in the mouth, so you don't have to remind me about it, but why the hell are you doing this? You're the predator who hunts companies like mine down and tears it to pieces."

In all honesty, I'm not even sure why I'm doing this. It's a huge risk, handing over this much money to a business that has already proven it's not exactly adept at keeping its head above water - but the thought of just leaving a proud old family business to sink even though it would be so easy to turn the company around - suddenly seems so wrong.

I might not have had this kind of help when I was getting started, but Christ, I'd have given just about everything to have a little hint of it. I have always been reluctant about helping out people in similar situations as me, just because I felt like I had to work so damn hard and long for whatever I got, why should I make it easy for anyone else?

But that was before I met Scarlett and found out that life is not all about profit. Recently, her voice is always at the back of my head, asking me if this is the kindest, or the most useful thing I could do, given the circumstance.

I know Tom Bilson's business hasn't failed yet, and with my help, there's a good chance that they'll stay afloat and even thrive.

"Hello?"

Tom's voice draws my attention again. I snap back to reality. "Yeah, I'm still here. I guess you can just put in down to the fact that you got me at a good time. But of course, I'll expect to be paid back with interest, and I wouldn't say no to stock either."

"Well, sure as heck you'll get paid back in both cash and stock!" he exclaims.

I can hear the giddiness in his voice. When I first heard him speak, he sounded like a man with a noose around his neck. Now, he is suddenly full of confidence and hope again.

I know that I'm the one who made the difference. I could have just sat back, let his company fail and feast on the carcass, but I didn't. And I am proud of myself. A warmth spreads through my chest when I think of recounting the story to Scarlett. I wonder what she'll say to me. "Right, I gotta go, but speak to my PA and get him to arrange a meeting for us this week," I tell him.

"I'll do that," he replies. "And... thank you. Thank you so very much. You have no idea how much this is going to mean to my family."

"No problem," I reply awkwardly. I'm not used to being on the receiving end of gratitude, that's for sure.

I hang up and call down to accounting. I'm going to have to make some moves with the money I promised him. It still feels strange and unfamiliar, but there is a sureness in my mind that tells me this is the right thing to do.

CHAPTER 29

SCARLETT

I smooth out my skirt and check my shoes for what feels like the dozenth time. I can hear Molly's voice in my head, telling me that I look great, but I'm not sure I believe her. I'm not sure I'll ever believe her, to be honest, not when it comes to dealing with people for whom clothes are an industry.

It's my first official meeting with Mark, and I feel like I am going to puke with nervousness. Zach offered to come along with me, but I turned him down. I figure it's time to strike out on my own and prove I can do this without him.

Which I know I can. I know I can!

I had a whole life before him, I have to keep reminding myself, and I got along just fine without him there by my side. Sometimes, it is easy to forget that, given how much a part of my life he has become since we got married. I know our marriage is only for show, but still... it's nice having someone around who I know has my corner.

Even if it's just until he gets what he wants from me.

I knock on the door. I then notice the way that Mark's receptionist is staring at me.

She's a slightly older woman. Her lips are a little pursed as she eyes me.

I wonder if it's to do with my outfit. I look away from her, trying to keep my cool. I don't feel like I'm doing a very good job. In fact, as I hear him moving around the office, my heartbeat picks up to near-fatal levels. I take a deep breath, and manage to smile when he opens the door.

"Scarlett, great to see you." He comes forward and does his usual, kiss on each cheek. Then, he steps aside to wave me in. He closes the door behind me as I take in his office.

It's large, airy and decked out with tasteful art and ultra-modern, uncomfortable looking silver furniture. I suppose he's got to sell the whole fantasy of his luxe lifestyle to anyone walking in here.

"Great to see you too, Mark," I reply.

"Take a seat," he invites, gesturing at the nest of sofas close by.

I perch at the edge of one of the sofas. I was right it is uncomfortably hard. "Thanks for agreeing to see me again so quickly, you must be so busy..."

"Never too busy to look into working with a great young talent like you," he replies, with a wide smile.

I am never sure how to respond to compliments, so I just offer a light laugh and hope it's enough for him.

"I thought we could talk about the particulars of what you

were going to be doing when you're working for me," he explains.

To my surprise, he doesn't take the seat at a desk or anything like I was expecting, but next to me on the same small sofa. It throws me off, but I don't let it show on my face. This must be normal. Fashion people are always a little kooky. Maybe I'm going to have to adopt a similar super-friendly demeanor and start kissing people twice on the cheeks if I'm going to make it in this world, too.

"I would love to hear about what you have in mind," I say with a smile as I pull a notebook and pen out of my bag. I really brought it along to take notes, but it also has a few of my sketches in it and if he happens to ask about those, too, then I suppose it's good to have them on hand...

"Oh, you don't need that," he tells me, reaching over, and closing the notebook.

I furrow my brow at him. "I would prefer to keep it around, if it's all the same—"

"And I'd prefer if you didn't, if it's all the same to you. I like to keep things just between us. I find notebooks and recording machines pesky things," he continues in a friendly voice.

I feel a shiver running down my spine, and I get the feeling that something is off. Maybe I should have listened to Zach. Maybe he knew something I didn't.

"I'm sure you understand the nature of this business," he goes on, speaking slowly, as though he's not sure that I am getting all of this. "That there's a lot of give and take between creatives..." He lets the words hang in the air between us.

I eye him expressionlessly. I have to give him the benefit of the doubt for now, as I'm not sure what other choice I have. If I get up and leave now, I'm not only going to blow my chances with this business, but he's a powerful man and he might blow any chance I have of making it in this industry.

"So..." he says with a slippery smile, "I need to know that you're going to be on board for that." Without warning, his hand slips from my notebook onto my knee, where he rests it firmly.

I look at his hand for a second, then back up to his face. "Of course, I'm happy to share ideas with you," I reply.

"And what about more than ideas?" he presses, as his hand inches a little further up my thigh.

Okay, now... I know something is wrong. I get to my feet quickly and turn away from him, managing to keep a smile on my face even though I feel like turning around and screaming at him. "What? Like portfolios? Tips on new designers?" I ask, holding my notebook out in front of me protectively. As though it's going to do anything to keep him away.

He rises to his feet to match me.

I fight the urge to shove him away from me.

"I was thinking more like beds," he murmurs.

I suppose in his head it might have sounded seductive, but it sounds so ridiculous coming out of his mouth that I nearly burst out laughing. Or, at least, I would have, if it hadn't been for the way he is looking at me, like a side of meat he can't wait to get his teeth into.

"I think you might have gotten the wrong idea about this," I tell him quickly, stepping away from him even as he advances on me. I think back to the look that the secretary gave me when I was entering this office, and I wonder if it might have had anything to do with what he is trying to pull on me right now. Has he done this before? Enough times for it to become a pattern? If he tries anything, I swear, I'll knee the slimeball in the crotch.

"Or maybe you have," he shoots back, a sharp edge to his voice.

I lift my hand, flashing my ring at him. "I'm married. And my husband is a very powerful man—"

"Oh, I know Zach," he replies, brushing off the warning. "Everybody knows about Zachary Black. He's not going to mind if you have a bit of fun, he's probably having some right now."

Okay, with that, I am done. A flood of rage rushes through me as I head for the door. I don't care if I never get a job in this industry, but I won't spend another second in this odious man's presence.

But as soon as I put my hand on the doorknob, I realize that the door to the office is locked.

CHAPTER 30

SCARLETT

My stomach drops and I turn back to him. "Unlock this door," I order. I'm so furious my voice is shaking. I wrap my arms around my notebook and glare at him, hoping I can spook him, but he doesn't seem bothered.

"Come on, you can't tell me that the thought hasn't crossed your mind," he tells me, sliding up next to me.

He's so close I catch a whiff of his gross aftershave once more. I draw my head away and do my best to stem the panic threatening to take me over. "If you don't let me out I'll scream," I threaten.

He laughs. "Scream away. This office is sound-proofed." He moves fast. Reaching for my shirt, he pulls down the edge of it to expose my shoulder.

Before I can jump away, I feel his teeth on my skin. And suddenly, something snaps inside me. I've spent so long without any control over my life, over myself, over my father's estate. Well, I'm not without control here.

I lift my hand and land a sharp—much sharper than what I gave Victoria—slap on his face.

Mark pulls back, his jaw hanging open. He clearly wasn't expecting that. "What the fuck?" he splutters, taking a step back from me.

My shoulder is throbbing where he just bit it, and I pull up my shirt to cover myself once more. "Unlock this door right now," I order. "Or I'll be kneeing you in the balls next." I have the upper hand now. I can get out of here. I *can* make him release me.

"If you walk out of here, I'm not going to support anything you do," he tells me. His face is burning-red where it had contact with me.

I can tell no one has done this to him before. Anyone he ever got in here was so desperate to work in the industry that they let him get away with it.

He is so livid he is glaring at me with pure hatred.

I don't care. I want him to feel as mad and humiliated as I did when he had me cornered. "I wouldn't expect less from you," I shoot back. "Now let me out."

"I'll tell everyone you're nothing more than a wannabe rich bitch who doesn't know a thing about fashion," he threatens, and he seems to be getting something out of being cruel.

It should sting, hearing those words, but I don't let them sink in. I no longer care about his opinion. He has already proved to me that he is the last man on Earth that I should be turning to for help. If he thinks I'm going to fall over myself to get his approval now, he must be crazy.

"Good," I snap back. "I don't want anyone thinking I have anything to do with you."

"Get the fuck out of here," he snarls, and pulling open the door, he practically shoves me outside.

I feel like I have just staged a prison break. I catch my breath, and notice his secretary giving me that look, the same one she had hit me with when I had walked in here. Pity. I didn't guess this before. I purse my lips and head for the door. If she's happy working for a man like that, then she's welcome to carry on. I have better things to do with my time.

As I drive back, I can feel a rush of emotion taking me over. Not just the release of all the adrenalin that had been swimming around my system, but something more than that. Sadness. Grief. I really thought that I had found a way into the industry. I was so desperate for that opportunity that I had deliberately blinded myself to all the clues Mark had been giving out. Now he had just underlined to me that a career in fashion was never going to happen to someone like me unless I was willing to whore myself and give in to the whims of the awful men who play gatekeeper in the industry.

How many women had walked in there, feeling just as hopeful as I did, only to walk out with the sense that everything they had clung to had been crushed? It isn't fair. And I don't feel like I should have to stand for it.

By the time I arrive home, I am crying. I try to pull myself together, not wanting to tell Zach what happened or have him get mad on my behalf. But as soon as I step over the threshold and see him standing there, his face full of worry.

CHAPTER 31

SCARLETT

He hurries towards me and wraps his arms around me just as I sink to the ground. He sinks down with me. "Hey, hey, what's wrong?" he asks, stroking my hair. "Did the meeting go badly?"

I can't reply. I am crying too hard. It takes me a moment to catch my breath and look up at him, and when I do, I can tell that he already knows what happened at the meeting.

"Your shirt," he murmurs, as he gently peels back the shoulder, the same shoulder that this awful man had sunk his teeth into. He pauses for a moment, taking in the teeth marks on my skin, and then his gaze finds mine. "Are you all right?" he asks gently.

I still can't say anything, but I look up at him and shake my head.

His face darkens. I can see the fury there; a towering rage I have never seen in his eyes before. And I know under no circumstances is he going to let this slide. He is going to make Mark pay dearly for what he did to me.

"I knew he was going to do something like this, I knew it," he mutters, as he clasps me tight and rocks me like a mother rocking her child. "But I clenched my teeth and let you go because I could see how desperate you were for this opportunity. I prayed I was wrong or at the very least, he would be smart enough not to try it with you."

"I'm sorry I didn't believe—you," I whisper brokenly.

"He's never going to do anything like this again, not to you, not to anyone else, don't you worry," he promises, getting to his feet and taking me with him.

Arnold has come running to see what is happening, his face full of concern.

"Arnold, can you get a car ready for me, please?" Zach asks.

"Yes, Sir," he says immediately, and turns away.

"Where are you going?" I ask Zach.

His mouth is set into a hard line. "I won't be long. Just wait for me, okay."

"You're not going to his office, are you? Please don't go, Zach. I don't want you getting in trouble for this! I just want to leave it all behind me."

"I'm not going to be able to leave this until I teach him a lesson he'll never forget and I know for damn certain that he's never going to do this to anyone else," he growls. "And I'm going to make sure the world knows the kind of narcissistic piece of shit he is. If you want to watch me do that, then by all means, come down with me."

I rise to my feet, and wipe my tears away with the back of my hand. "That actually sounds good," I say, and I mean it. Zach is right. He should be humiliated by someone more powerful than him. He should be hurt the same way he hurt me and the whole world should know that he is a monster preying on young women's dreams of entering the industry. Like Zach, I want to make sure that he never does what he tried to do to me to anyone again.

I curl up in the front seat of the car while Zach drives. My tears have dried, at least for now, because I know that Mark is going to get what is coming to him. If anyone can make him pay for what he's done, it's Zach. Zach is just as powerful in business as he is.

We get to Mark's office building and Zach gets out of the car.

I hesitate. I thought I wanted to see Mark get bloodied, but in fact, I don't want to watch it go down. Also, I can't bear to set foot inside that building again. "I think I'm going to stay here," I tell Zach "Is that okay?"

"Anywhere you feel safe," he replies, then impulsively, he leans over and kisses me on the lips.

I know he is doing this for me. He is doing this because he can't bear to see me in pain. Because he is my husband, because maybe, just maybe he... he cares about me. The thought makes my skin prickle and my hair stand on end.

"This won't take long," he tells me then he stalks into the building.

I let my gaze travel up to the ceiling to floor windows that looks into the waiting room of Mark's office.

I can't hear anything from inside the car, but after a while, I see Zach brushing through the room and into Mark's office. The secretary gets to her feet, in a vague attempt to stop him, but he doesn't seem to even notice her. I am so proud that he is my man. I can't think of many people out there who would feel bold enough or brave enough to strike out on behalf of me, but there he is, making his stand for me.

Another minute passes. And then, there is a commotion.

Mark, bloodied, stumbles away from his office. He is clutching his face like he is in serious pain. Looks like Zach did more than just land a slap on him. Zach storms out after him, flexing his fingers like he is ready to hit him again. Mark shouts at him and backs away. Even from this distance, I can see what a coward he is. He looks terrified. I can't make out what they're saying, of course, but I don't need to. All that I need to know is that Mark has paid for what he did to me.

A few more minutes pass, then Zach appears outside the car once more. Though his knuckles are bloodied, there is a grin on his face. He looks like a schoolboy, fresh from the fight.

"Did you really just...?" I ask as he climbs back into the car.

"Hit him hard enough that I think he lost a few teeth?" He grins at me. "Yeah, I think so. And I told him that I'm going to expose him. I'm going to get a few lawyers on the case, see who I can get to speak up. I'm sure there are lots of women with stories to tell. That secretary of his seemed pretty keen to share something with me. Fuck knows what she's seen over the years..."

He grabs the steering wheel and winces.

I reach out to caress his sore hand. I can't believe that he stood up for me. Without even thinking twice. This isn't the Zach that I knew all those weeks ago, the Zach who I had written off in my head as selfish, cruel, and sleazy. "Here, let me drive," I suggest.

He shakes his head, but I'm not taking no for an answer.

"Come on, I think it's the least I can do after you just defended my honor like that," I tease. "Let me drive us home? And maybe make you dinner tonight."

He glances at me and grins. "I suppose I could swing that," he agrees, and shifts from the driver's seat to allow me to take the wheel.

Before pulling away, I look over at him one more time. "And thank you again," I tell him. "For defending me like that. You have no idea how much better I feel, knowing that he's not going to be able to do that to other women."

"No he won't," he states fervently.

I know he means it. Zach isn't the kind of man who does things by halves, that is what I have discovered above all else in the time I have known him. He is many things, but he is not a faker. He might have thought he was, when it came to our marriage, but I can see through that now. I can see that he wants to protect me the way a real husband would. And I know that everything I have been feeling for him, he feels it right back.

I pull out of the parking lot, and I finally let myself smile. I can take on anything as long as I have him by my side.

It is the only thing that matters.

CHAPTER 32

ZACH

"**W**hat are you saying?" I demand, leaning forward and narrowing my eyes at Scarlett's family lawyer, Ernest.

He pushes his glasses up his nose and uselessly shuffles the documents in front of him. "Look, I was sure this was going to work too." He raises his eyebrows at me pointedly. "But it turns out you're not the most popular man in town, Zach. Seems like it's gone against you in this instance."

I lean back in the chair and stare at him. After all Scarlett has done, it is possible that she won't get the one thing I know she wants above all else. I glance over at her, and her face is set with tension. I don't blame her. She must feel this like a punch to the gut. That's certainly how it feels to me.

I'd felt so sure this would work. In fact, there should have been no reason that it didn't. This is what I am struggling with. I have spent so long trying to figure out the details of how best to approach this that by the time we put in the request, I was dead certain I had everything on lockdown. As it turns out, though... I am wrong. And it's all because my fucking reputation got in the way of the one thing Scarlett truly wanted from me.

"Can you explain what's going on?" Scarlett asks.

I almost wince as I can hear her voice trembling.

"Scarlett, we put in the request to have the property expedited to you and Zach, but it doesn't look like you're going to be able to get hold of it," Ernest explains to her gently. "I know it's what you wanted, but the judge who looked over the case denied it."

"On what grounds?" I demand. "Everything was in order... there was no good reason—"

"Seems like you picked off the carcass of the business of one of his brothers," Ernest says, a spiky edge to his voice.

He blames me for this.

I shake my head in disbelief. Of course, just as I start to change my tune and focus on something more positive for my business, my previous practices come swinging in to bite me in the ass and remind me of the jerk-off I've been.

"Oh, my God," Scarlett gasps. Her face is as white as a sheet, and she looks as though she is about to pass out.

"Here, take a drink," Ernest says kindly, and pushes a glass of water over the table towards her.

She grabs it and takes a sip, but it doesn't do much to help. She closes her eyes for a moment and takes a deep breath. "So you're telling me that we're not going to be able to get the house back from Victoria?" Her voice is high-pitched and panicky.

This isn't fair on her. This is all she wanted. She was willing to go to wild lengths, giving up all her shares she owned, marrying me, for fuck's sake, to get what she wanted. And now, it has blown up in her face. It kills me to think not only am I not going to be able to deliver my part of the bargain for her, it turns out it is my fault that she can't get the most important thing to her. I feel helpless, useless, and I hate myself for it.

"It doesn't look like this marriage is going to be the way to do it," he replies grimly. "You could approach her and offer to buy it outright, but... I doubt she'd hand over the place to you no matter how much money you offered her, anyway. Seems like she's got it out for you and Lori."

I reach out to take Scarlett's hand. She just lets hers sit limply in mine, not seeming to care one little bit about whether I'm there or not. I have never felt so terrible in my life. I have completely failed her, and I don't see any other way I can get her what she wants.

"Can you arrange a meeting with her?" I suggest. "Something soon? Let me talk it over with her, get her to see that—"

"You can't," Ernest replies. "She's on vacation."

"On vacation?" Scarlett spits.

I can hear the vitriol in her voice. There's no doubt in my mind that she really, *really* hates this woman. I don't blame her. She's a raging bitch keeping a house she doesn't even want from Scarlett just because she can. I don't know what kind of sick freak would get off on something like that.

"She's going to be out of the country for at least the next

month, and I think she fully expects to have sold the house by then," he explains. "She's had a few offers already..."

"A few offers?" Scarlett repeats blankly.

Ernest nods. "It's probably not going to be long until someone takes it," he tells her gently. "Perhaps you and Lori should prepare for the eventuality."

"I'm not preparing for anything," she replies, as she gets to her feet. She seems to sway unsteadily, making me jump to my feet too. "I don't see why I should have to give up my ancestral home just because Victoria is too much of a bitch to sell it to me. She doesn't even want it, and she won't even let us buy it back from her? What kind of—"

But before she can finish what she is saying, the blood drains from her face, as she tries to grab the back of the chair to try and keep herself upright. But her brain has already shut off and her body crumples beneath her.

I catch her before she hits the ground. "Open the window," I tell Ernest. "We need to get her some air. This is too stressful for her. I'm not surprised she went down..." I put Scarlett on the chair and hold her head between her knees. Silently, I apologize to her, over and over again, for failing her the way I have. I'm going to make it right. I'm going to find a way to make it right...

Within a few minutes, Scarlett comes around. As soon as she comes to, I see the distress come back into her eyes.

"I'm going to lose the house, Zach," she whispers and her eyes fill with tears.

Watching her cry has the strangest effect on me. It breaks me in a way I never thought possible. I scoop her into my arms and carry her to the car. I'm going to make it right. I'm going to find a way to make it right...

As I'm driving, and Scarlett is curled up on her seat and gazing out of the window. She hasn't said a word to me since she whispered that one heart-breaking statement. She doesn't need to. I can tell everything that's going through her head. She is so hurt, so hurt at the news that she will not get her family home back.

And it is all my fault.

She must blame me for it. I wish I could go to that judge, tell him the truth, that things are different now. That he doesn't know the half of who I am or what I'll become. But I know it doesn't work that way. He has made his mind up and the best I can do is start thinking of other ways I can approach this case and get Scarlett what she wants so badly.

We arrive at my doctor's office. I go around quickly to help her out of the car.

She leans on me heavily, as though she can barely stand or to keep herself upright under her own steam. She is utterly exhausted. Maybe it is the shock, but it seems strange that she could be weak.

I start to worry that something else might be wrong with Scarlett.

Dr. Dansen ushers us through to his office at once.

Scarlett sits on the edge of the hard bed as he checks her over and takes her blood.

I sit opposite her, urging her silently to look up at me, to give me some sign that she's not blaming me, but she stares straight ahead and answers all the doctor's questions robotically.

"Just give me a few moments to run your vitals and I'll be back with you," he tells us, and heads out of the office.

I reach over for Scarlett's hand and hold it tight.

She finally looks up at me. It is the first time she has acknowledged my presence in the room, and it seems like something of a relief to see me there.

"We'll find another way," I promise her. "We will. I don't care how long it takes, we'll find another way..."

"I don't know that we can," she replies quietly, like she has already come to that conclusion herself. "Maybe it's time to just—just..." she swallows hard as if she can't even say the words. "Let go. Move on." Silent tears well up in her eyes roll down her cheeks.

I wipe them away with my thumbs as I make a silent promise to myself. I don't care if I lose everything I have. I am going to get that house for her. "I don't want you to do that," I urge. "I want that girl back, the one who will never say die. Do you hear me? We'll find another way, I promise you. Just wait and you'll see. My father always said there's more way than one to skin a cat..."

Before she could reply, the doctor enters the room once more. He seems comfortable and pretty happy with the results he's looking at.

I am glad to see it. My wife has become my life now, and I can't imagine what I would do if there was something truly wrong with her.

"Everything seems to be just fine," the doctor tells us with a smile. "Mother and baby are just fine."

And with that, everything stops.

She freezes, and my mind actually goes blank. I can't think at all. I just stare at Dr. Dansen in open-mouthed shock.

"No, there must be some kind of mistake," Scarlett tells him as she manages a little splutter of laughter, even though there is no mirth at all to the sounds coming out of her mouth. "I'm not – I'm not pregnant. There is no baby. I'm on the pill..."

"Well, you must be carrying one of those miracle babies that just will not take no for an answer," the doctor says with a laugh. "Yes, I would say you're about a month along, by my estimation? You can get pregnant if you missed even one day or if you vomit."

He keeps talking, but everything else after that fades out to static in my brain. There's no way...she can't be. She just can't be. She's not meant to... we were just faking the marriage. The baby isn't fake. This is real, this is happening...

She is talking to him, as I tune back in. She is babbling, just trying to get the words out, "But I—I can't be that far along. I was only."

"If this is the first you're finding out about it, I suggest you and your husband take some time to talk over your options, and if you decide you want to move forward with the pregnancy, then I can refer you to some excellent ob-gyns."

"Yes, that would be great," I say.

He writes down some numbers for us and hands them over to me.

I take the page silently. I feel as if I am running on autopilot.

"Right, then. I wish you both the best of luck," the doctor says into the dense silence.

I help Scarlett to her feet and the two of us head back out to the car. The world feels like it is muted as we step back in together.

She closes the door behind her and stares off into space as if she is shell-shocked.

I know exactly how she feels. We've both just had the bomb-shell of a lifetime dropped on top of us.

"I didn't know," she blurts out finally. "You have to believe me, I had no idea. Really. It was—it was as much a shock to me as it was to you..."

"Yeah, I can tell that," I reply grimly. I don't know what I'm meant to say to her. I don't even know if she wants to keep the baby. *Our baby. Our baby.* And I know at that instant that I want it. More than she wants her house.

"I wouldn't have kept this from you," she continues fervently. "I—I would have told you the truth, if I had known. You understand that, right?"

"Yes, I know."

"Let's go home," she says. "I need to get some rest, don't you?"

"Yeah, I do," I agree as I start the car up and head towards home.

Suddenly out of nowhere, a happy little thought comes into my head. Soon, it won't just be ours. We have a little invader on the way.

CHAPTER 33

ZACH

"**E**xplain it to me one more time?" Tom Bilson asks me *again*.

The job doesn't require a business genius, but I can be patient with him. I have too much at stake not to get it right first time around. "Okay. Your company will buy the property from Victoria Johnson-Forger. And then you will sell it back to me, but at no time will you let her or any of her other associates know that you are a proxy buyer."

"As soon as I have the contracts signed, I call you and let you know, right?" he finishes.

"Exactly," I agree.

He eyes me from across the desk. "You sure about this? It seems like an odd way to repay you for the money."

"This is the only thing I need," I reply, and I mean it. "If you can get this for me, you have my ongoing support for as long as you need it. That's a promise."

Tom's face lights up. I know he is still getting over the fact that I offered him my support in the first place, but throwing this on top of it must be even more of a relief. His family business will be in the clear again, after looking like it was going to crash.

I just need his help to take care of some other family business, and this whole thing will be over.

"Alright, well, I'll let you know as soon as I've signed the contracts," he replies, getting to his feet and holding his hand out to me.

"Alright," I nod, and I shake his hand.

"I'll speak to you soon, okay?" he says before he heads to the door.

I sink back into my seat as soon as he is done and let out a long sigh. It feels like it has been a fury of work this past week even though I still have a few more steps to take before I make the land and house package mine for good.

I never imagined in a million years that I'd be a father, and I would be anything other than straight horrified at the prospect of it, but I'm not. I love the idea of being a father to our baby.

I haven't spoken to Scarlett about it though. I know that she needs time to process all the crazy things that are happening to her. She hasn't said she wants to keep it and I can't force her to keep it, but I don't think I will need to. I trust her. I know she could never kill our baby. What we made together. A miracle baby that survived against all odds.

I can't help but feel like this is some kind of fate. We are married, and now she is pregnant. That is how these things are supposed to be.

Being around her makes everything shine brighter, that's for sure. Life is just ten times better when she's with me... it's just that simple. Even though it might sound cheesy, and it is the kind of thing I would have internally rolled my eyes at if someone else had come at me with this story of me getting married and having a baby. Despite all that, it's the pure truth. It's not just that I enjoy being around her, but even when she's not by my side, I find myself thinking about her.

She doesn't even know that I've been helping out with Tom's company, but she will soon, and as soon as she does, she's going to know I did it for her.

I spend the rest of the day trying to distract myself and keep busy. I jump to answer the phone every time it rings, but it's never Tom. Not yet. As soon as he has the property under contract, then I know they are as good as mine. And there's no need for Victoria to hear a word about it.

I know that if I'm going to convince Scarlett to start a family with me, she's going to want to do it in the very same house she grew up in. That place is her family home, and every time she talks about it, I know she wants nothing more than to go back there and start her family there.

Finally, the phone rings. I snatch it up and I hear Tom's voice.

"Did you get it?" I ask.

He pauses for a moment, and I am sure he is going to tell me that he didn't. That somehow, Victoria saw through my plan, and refused to sell the house to him, even though his offer was higher than anything she had received until now.

"I got it!" he exclaims.

I swear, champagne corks pop and fireworks explode in my

head. I can't believe it. It really worked. "You got it?" I repeat, as a flood of relief rushes through me.

"I got it," he assures me. "And I'll come down with the deeds to your place as soon as I get the chance, and you can get it all signed over to you officially."

"Thank you so much," I tell him. "You have no idea how important this is to me—"

"You have no idea how important our business is to our family," he tells me with equal sincerity. "You're the one who saved our asses, Zachary Black. And we owe you big time."

"Well, consider the debt repaid," I tell him. "How long before you can get down here?"

"An hour, at most?"

"I'll get my lawyers up and we can get this on paper and finalized," I reply. "I'll see you soon, alright?"

I hang up the phone and allow myself a victorious air-punch. I'm still a bit wary that it all actually came through. But I suppose, the way to a gold digger's heart is always through a huge pile of cash. As long as she doesn't know I am behind the sale, it should all be smooth sailing. The old version of me would have balked at paying above the odds for anything, but there isn't any amount I wouldn't have paid to make sure that Scarlett got what she wanted.

Soon enough, Tom is at the office, and we run through all the legal proceedings to make sure that everything is as it should be. It all moves so fast and cements the idea in my head. Usually, when I get an idea in my head, it's impossible to get rid of it. And I have this idea, of Scarlett and I raising our little kid in Wotton House.

As soon as the contracts are signed, I head down to the car to make my way back home. Scarlett probably thinks I have been avoiding her, given all the time that I'd been staying at the office working out this deal, but when I show her what I've really been working on...

Fuck, I feel nervous. Really nervous. Because I want that dream of us living together and building our family, so badly.

CHAPTER 34

ZACH

I walk into the entrance hall, and head straight to the library, where I know she will be hiding out. Whenever she is stressed or worried, she hangs out in there. She has barely left the last week.

A few times, I have ducked my head inside and found her passed-out asleep on the chair, a book falling out of her hand. Then I have carried her to bed, carefully, at least three times this week, and she always nestles into my arms when I lift her out of the chair. As though she wants me, but hasn't been allowing herself that weakness.

"Scarlett?" I call as I step inside.

She looks over at me from one of the enormous chairs in the center of the room. She looks exhausted with her hair scraped back from her face and piled on her head, no make-up on, just wearing a robe and some slippers. She usually takes every chance she gets to get dressed up and show off her inimitable fashion sense, but she hasn't been able to muster the energy for it.

"Hey, Zach," she replies, her voice lackluster.

I make my way over to join her, sitting down in the chair next to her and planting the briefcase with the deeds in it at my feet. "I need to talk to you," I tell her.

She bites her lip and nods. "Yeah, I figured you would," she murmurs, and she looks away from me. "Let's just get this over with, huh?"

"Get what over with?" I ask, confused.

"I know that you don't want any of this," she says sadly. She can't even look me in the eyes. "I know that you didn't—you never signed up to have a baby. Or to have to deal with me. You did this so you could get your hands on the land and I could get the house, and now it's this whole... fucking mess and you probably just want out, don't you?"

"You think I'm here because I want to end things?" I ask incredulously.

Scarlett nods. "So let's just get this over with and we can stop pretending," she tells me, and she lets her hand rest on her stomach. "I can do this by myself. I know I can."

I take her chin in my fingers and force her to look at me. "Oh, my darling Scarlett. Listen to me. I didn't come here because I want to break things off with you."

She stares at me, her breath catching. Her eyes filling with hope and yet afraid it is all some twisted joke. "Then what are you doing here?"

Her voice is so tiny and nervous it makes my heart ache. I reach down to the briefcase I have with me and unclip it, then I pull out the papers inside. "Here you go," I murmur as I hand the deeds over to her.

Her eyes skim down the pages in front of her, and it takes her a moment to register what they are. Her eyes widen, and then it seems to hit her. "These are—"

"—the deeds for Wotton Hall, your rightful inheritance," I finish up for her. "Along with the land and the woods around it. Everything. I got it for you, Scarlett."

She stares at me for a long while.

I can't read the expression on her face. Is she happy? Sad? Confused? I reach out to touch her cheek.

She leans her face into my hand. "H-how did you get these?" she asks. "Is it—was it legal?"

"It's all legal," I promise. "I've been working with this company, a family business, giving them some guidance to get back on their feet after a bad few years. They brought the lands for me and then I purchased it from them. They belong to me now, Scarlett. To us."

She doesn't say a word, her eyes are still locked on the pages in front of her. When she eventually raises them, she looks at me with confusion. "And what does this mean? For—for us? If we both got what we wanted..." She trails off.

I am surprised that she still has doubts after all this time, but I will do everything I can to make sure I put them to rest. "I want to live there with you," I explain to her. "Raise our baby there with you, if you'll have me."

"You do?" she gasps. "Oh, God, I can't believe this! I never thought—I thought you were totally freaked out when the doctor told us I was pregnant. I thought you didn't want anything to do with me or the baby."

"I was freaked out," I admit. "But in the nicest way possible. Being with you has changed me, Scarlett. I think you've turned me into the kind of man who can actually stand up and take responsibility for what matters. And this is what matters to me. You matter to me. You both do."

"Oh, Zach. This isn't a dream, is it? I'm not going to wake up and…"

I reach out and cover the hand that is on her stomach and smile. A tear rolls down her cheek, and I brush it away with my thumb. "Hey."

More tears roll down her cheeks.

"Are you okay?"

"I think so," she murmurs. "This just—it's more than I expected, that's all."

"You really thought I was just going to walk out on you, after everything we've been through together?" I ask her.

She lowers her gaze and shakes her head. "I was scared. I hoped of course, but I didn't want to be disappointed. I've been so disappointed in my life. So many things I wanted were snatched away from me," she explains. "I knew that I—I knew how I felt about you, but I couldn't be sure how you felt about me. I kept wondering if I'd made it all up in my head."

"You didn't make it up, not any of it," I promise her fervently. "Scarlett, I love you." As soon as the words were out of my mouth, I knew I had reached the point of no return. There would be no coming back from this, not from the reality of knowing that yes, I was truly, deeply and madly in love with her.

Her eyes widen, as she claps her hand over her mouth and then laughs delightedly. "Oh my God, Zach!" she screams.

"I think the generally-accepted reaction is to say it back," I remark with a smile.

Scarlett clasps my face in her hands and looks deep into my eyes. "I love you, too, Zachary Winston Black. I love you so much, I could die with love," she tells me.

"Don't you dare do that," I say and kiss her, softly, on the mouth. This is how it started, how it all started. With a kiss. With knowing that as soon as I kiss her, I won't be able to stop there.

I reach over and pull her on to my lap, wrapping my arms around her. God, I love this woman so much. I want everything with her. And I have known that for a long time, even if I have only just come to terms with it now. The way she tastes, the way she moves, the way she smiles, kisses, fucks, all of it.

I need it all.

She spreads her legs to straddle me.

I pull her robe open and let it slide off her to the floor below. Underneath she is naked, so beautifully naked, and something about her shyness feels as if she is baring herself to me for the very first time, and I am seeing her, truly seeing her for the first time too. I love the way she looks, the way she feels.

This woman is everything to me. The mother of my child. My wife. The love of my life, and more than that, the woman who changed me. She made me into the version of me that I thought I would never be, a version that moves through the world with kindness and decency. The kind of man that a woman could actually imagine raising a child with.

I lower my mouth to her breast and flick my tongue out over her nipple, filling myself with the sweet taste of her, as I slide my hands around her waist. I'm going to allow myself to get lost in her in a way I never have before.

She reaches down and slides her hands over my cock, through my pants. Expertly, she pulls me out and strokes me a few times, even though I am already rock hard for her. She plants one hand on the chair behind me and uses the other to guide me inside of her.

As soon as she does this, I close my eyes and let out a long groan of pleasure. "Fuck, yes," I growl, as I grasp her hips to pull her down onto me harder. I love the way she feels. So soft, so wet, and so inviting. This body belongs to me. I slide my hand over her cheek and caress her skin, watching as the glint of my ring plays off the light around us. She draws my fingers into her mouth, and I watch as she coaxes them in, trailing her tongue around my fingertips.

One of the staff could walk in on us at any moment, but I'm finding it pretty hard to give a damn. How can I care about that, when all that matters is the way she is looking down at me, like I am the most important thing in the world to her?

She closes her eyes, tips her head back. and lets me impale her.

I thrust up and into her, filling her with my whole length at once. Once I have built up a pace, she starts to move and grind her clit against me. I know what she's asking for. I slide my hand down from her throat to her breasts to her belly and lower, till my fingers are grazing over her clit.

"Oh," she moans, as she moves up my shaft and slams back down a little harder.

I can tell from the look on her face that she is getting close and I want, more than anything to see her give herself to me. I need to see it. She sinks her fingers into my shoulders and clutches on to me tight as she goes harder, faster, her hips moving like she is possessed by the urge to release...

"Ah!" she cries out, as she tips her head back and allows her orgasm to take over.

The feeling of her pussy clenching around my bare cock is almost enough to push me over the edge right then and there, but I am not ready yet. I want to commit this moment to memory, the way she feels, the way she looks, the way it makes me feel.

I hold on to her hips and keep her in place, watching the way her breasts sway as she slowly grinds on top of me, over and over again, guiding the last vestiges of pleasure from me before she is good and done.

When I let myself come, it feels like I am letting out a breath I had been holding for decades. It is more than just the orgasm, more than just the simple act of her giving herself to me. It is something more profound. It is passion, pleasure, promise, the reality of what we have shared and what we will share in the future. I tip her head down to face mine and lean up to kiss her as we both come back down to the real world together.

Scarlett unwinds herself from me, grabs her robe and drapes it over my lap so she can settle down comfortably. She lets out a cute little giggle.

"What is it?" I ask, nuzzling her neck. I want to find out every detail about her, about her past, about the way she feels and thinks. I am still fascinated by this woman. I love her so much. I know I will never get enough.

"I was just thinking that we're already husband and wife," she points out. "I like that. We don't have to worry about living in sin or having a child out of wedlock or anything like that."

"That doesn't strike me as the kind of thing you would be much worried about anyway," I remark.

She rests her head on my shoulder. "You're right," she replies. "I don't care. As long as you're here."

I place a gentle kiss on her temple. I know just how she feels. I could have stayed here all night long if she'd wanted me to, just holding her and our baby in my arms. I let my eyes drift shut to savor the sensation… the rest of the world can wait, as I hold the woman I love tight in my arms.

CHAPTER 35

"Are you sure about this?" Molly asks, fretfully.

I glance over my shoulder at her. "About what?" For a moment, I think she is about to cast doubt on the vow renewal I am about to commit to with the man I love, but I know she isn't that stupid. If she'd had issues, she would have told me about them before this moment.

But of course, she is just checking out the shoes she is wearing with her sweet blue dress, checking them out in the mirror. "About the shoes, that's all," she replies, glancing up at me and smiling. "Did you think I was talking about you and your husband-to-be?"

"He's already my husband," I point out.

She smiles at me. "Yeah, but you know what I mean," she replies. "He's going to be your *husband* now. Not just on paper."

"Yeah, I get what you mean," I reply with a smile and nod to her shoes. "I think they look good, don't stress about them."

"That's easy for you to say when you look so incredible," she says.

I check myself out in the mirror. I designed this outfit from scratch and I'm happy with how it turned out. More flattering over my baby bump. It has cream panels and deep charcoal accents. It might be a little more traditional than the suit I wore to our first marriage, but this is different. This is real.

It's the first dress that I've put together in a few months; after what happened with Mark, I was nervous about moving forward with any of my ideas. No matter how much Zach encouraged me, I was just frightened about the same thing happening again. I remember how desperate I was for that job. I was so desperate I even fooled myself into not believing Zach.

"You can't let what that asshole did to you get in the way of you living your life," he told me, more times than I could count. "You've got real talent. You should get out there and show the world just how good you are."

"I don't know about that," I replied, turning my face away from him. "When the baby comes—"

"When the baby comes, I'm sure you're not going to want to sit on your butt all day doing nothing, right? You're going to want to have a life. You should get some of your designs out there."

"I don't know where I'd even start..."

"You can do it," he encouraged. "You want to change the industry, right? Make it so that guys like Mark can't just do what they want whenever they want?"

"I guess so," I admitted. I had been doing some research, and had found that a lot of women had experiences similar to mine. Not just with Mark, either, but with other men in the business. It really grossed me out, but I didn't know how to change it.

"You have money, you have influence, you have talent," he reminded me. "Get back to designing. See where it takes you, okay?"

"Easy for you to say—"

"Easy for me to say because I believe that you're totally capable of it," he replied. "You know I don't invest in people I don't believe in."

"I don't think a marriage is the same as an investment," I teased.

"I would disagree," he replied, with a grin. "But don't worry, I've heard the returns are excellent..."

What happened after that was somewhat a blur to me, but he certainly distracted me from the conversation at hand. But he had switched on a thought in my head, one I didn't want to drop.

I started looking into beginning my own business. I knew it was a big leap, and that my skills didn't really extend to running a place of my own, but I didn't need to shoot for the stars on my first time around so I registered a company, with the help of my supportive husband, of course, and started designing. Right now, we are a small operation. Well, it's just me designing and sewing, as well as a couple of girls who are visiting local stores to scout out potential homes for our designs, but I'll get there. I know I will.

"You think you're ready? I mean... to go out there?" Molly asks.

I bite my lip and run my hands over my pregnancy bump. I look so big in the mirror. I think I like the way I look, but it's hard to tell when I feel so clumsy and ungainly. "I think so," I reply. "Are you sure I don't look too whale-like in this dress?"

Molly is instantaneous in her opposition to my idea. "Are you mad?" she exclaims. "You've never looked more beautiful. And Zach is going to think you look amazing."

I smile at her in the mirror. Thank God, she is here to keep me sane.

Speaking of keeping me sane, Lori bursts through the door, practically out of breath. She has been so excitable with the marriage and baby announcement that she has been driving me a little crazy. Even so, I get it. This is an expansion to our family, after all this time. So she's allowed to feel excited about it

"Hey, are you ready to go out there?" she asks excitedly. "I think you should. The place is already full, everyone's waiting for you..."

"Well, I guess I've got no more excuses to hang around here, huh?" I try to sound upbeat about it, but I'm nervous. I am excited of course, to renew my vows with my amazing husband, but this time it's for real. I was less worried the last time about falling over in front of his whole family or something, as they weren't even there. This time around? Yeah, you could say I'm pretty freaked about it.

"No more excuses," Lori says, offering me her hand. "Come on, I'm giving you away, right?"

"I think I am," Molly shoots back, and she takes my other hand.

"Ladies, ladies," I joke. "There's enough of me to go around." I gesture to my tummy.

"Not after he sweeps you off on your honeymoon," Lori mocks. "You have to send me pictures every day, okay? I want to see everything. I wish I could come out to Thailand with you."

"You should, one day," I suggest. "Could be fun."

"Girl's trip!" Molly squeals.

I laugh. I am so glad they're here for me today. I don't think I would have been able to make it through this day without feeling like I'm going to burst with nerves. "Okay, stop distracting me, you two," I tease. "Let's get out of here."

With that, we head out of the dressing room and down to the church, where my husband is waiting for me.

Zach was the one who insisted on a proper church wedding. I told him that I really didn't care if we got remarried again or not, but he told me he wanted to start over properly. I appreciated his commitment to a clean start, so I went with it. And honestly, I have been looking forward to this for months. It's a chance for us to leave all the bad things that happened behind us and move forward together, as a unit. As a family.

I am only a few months from my due date, and I had insisted that we get this done before the kid made an appearance.

We've decided not to find out the gender, keeping it as a surprise for now, but I have a feeling it's going to be a girl.

Either way, I know that we are going to be far too busy when she or he comes along to think about throwing a wedding, and besides, I want us to commit to each other before we commit to this child.

His family is here. Thank goodness, they like me. We decided to mention as little as possible about the truth of how we ended up together in the first place. A few papers reached out to us in the hopes of getting a scoop, but we want to keep it to ourselves. This is just about us, not anyone else. Showing that we love each other, and we want all the important people in our lives to know about it.

Sometimes, I still can't quite believe I'm with Zach. Sometimes, I wake up in the morning and just watch him sleep. Never in a million years had I imagined a man like Zach would ever settle down, let alone with a woman like me. I'd been a virgin when we met, but I don't care to know anything more of the world of sex and romance than what he can show me. This man is my past, my present, and my future.

The harpist we chose for the ceremony strikes up as I enter the grand hall of the church. It is dappled with a gorgeous golden light, sparkling everywhere I look, but all I can see is him.

Zach is smiling at me like I am the most beautiful thing he has ever seen in his life.

All the nerves fall away, and I hope that, somewhere, my mother and father are looking down on me, glad that I have chosen to share my life and their old home with a man who loves me so much. Sometimes, I think my dad knew exactly what he was doing when he left the house in Victoria's name, but made sure Zach and I would hold the controlling interest if we joined up and got married. I'll never forget his words on his dying bed, when he said, *'I love you, Scarlett my darling. You are my first born and have always been my favorite. I have set it up so that you will be safe from this cruel world.'*

This is what he'd meant. Somehow, he knew Ernest would remember about the shares Zach owned. Then the fact that he had sold Zach those shares with no real reason to have even done so... I believe he had it all set up. So I would have this day when I married Zachary Winston Black for real.

I meet Zach at the end of the aisle, as Lori and Molly fall into place behind me. I smile at him, and he takes my hand.

"You ready?" he asks

I am so happy—I can't speak. I nod.

"Then I'll begin," announces the priest.

Zach squeezes my hand tight, and I squeeze back. The sunlight streaming in warms my body, and I know that everything is right now. Everything is exactly as it should be.

I am safe from the cruel world.

EPILOGUE

SCARLETT

Almost six years later

I lie on the cool grass of the peaceful little cemetery where all my ancestors are buried and look up at the sky. It is going to be a fine day. Already the summer sun is filtering through the trees in the woods.

"Happy Birthday, Mom," I whisper.

A gentle breeze answers me and makes me smile. I know the breeze has nothing to do with Mom, but somehow it makes me feel as if she is in that breeze. She is watching and she is happy that I kept my promise to her. I turn my head and see Dad's tombstone next to mom's.

A year after Florence was born, I was in his study going through his papers when to my shock, I found a letter from him to me. His words are burned in my memory.

· · ·

Hello Darling,

If you have found this letter it means my little plan worked, and you know that wherever I am, I'm chuckling to myself. I always was a smug bastard!

But isn't he just the perfect husband for you?

I died easy because I knew he would protect and take care of you until his last breath. Actually, I always knew he was the right man for you. From the first moment I introduced him to you, but I didn't want him to have you too young. It is the nature of youth not to appreciate life's gifts so I kept him away. If not for my early demise I would have made him wait another two years, but what can you do. Death and taxes...

Well, my darling, there is no more to say, except I love you and I'll be the butterfly that alights on your hand, the breeze that lifts your hair away from your cheek to caress your skin, the snow crunching under your feet. No matter where you look, I'll be there watching you and doing everything a spirt can to protect you.

Until we meet again, be happy always, Scarlett my love.

. . .

A s I close my eyes to remember my father, I hear a shout. Lifting my head, I see my daughter, Florence running towards me. In the sunlight, her hair glows like a golden halo around her head. She is holding a flower in her hand. I sit up and wait for her.

"I brought a flower for Nana," she shouts, holding up the flower. She has squeezed the stalk so hard it is broken.

I hide a smile. My daughter is so cute I want to bite her. "That's nice."

She stomps up to me and sticks her abused flower in the vase with the flowers I brought. "Happy Birthday, Nana," she says solemnly.

For a while I stay silent and allow her words to fill the air.

"Where's Daddy," I ask.

"Making pancakes."

"You mean you walked all the way here by *yourself?*"

She shrugs casually. When she does that she reminds me so much of Zach. That is exactly how he shrugs. "I took the shortcut."

My jaw drops. "Through the woods?"

"Yes," she confirms proudly.

I frown. "I don't want you walking through the woods by yourself."

"Daddy said I could."

"Well, I'm going to have to speak to him about that because —," I stop as another gust of wind blows hair into my face. I look at my daughter's innocent eyes. Now is not the time to scold her. Not here where my parents rest in peace. "Flo, do you know that one day," I make a sweeping gesture with my hand, "all this will be yours."

Her eyes widen. "All of it?"

"Yes. All of it."

She tilts her head. "But what about Brandon? I don't think he'll like that."

"Brandon will get Daddy's house."

"Oh!" She thinks about it for a moment. "Is Daddy's house bigger?"

"Yes."

She nods slowly. "That's all right then, because Brandon always wants the bigger piece."

I smile. "That's true, but the thing is this house has been in Mommy's family for six hundred years, and it has been always passed down through the girls. So after me it will be your turn to have the house."

"Okay, Mommy." She jumps up. "Now can we go back. I don't want Brandon to eat *all* the pancakes."

I get to my feet and together we walk back through the woods. We take the footpath hidden by the big hedges and go into the house through the kitchen door.

Zach is busy at the stove. No one can rock an apron like him.

He looks up when we enter, his face breaking in a large grin. "Just in time."

"Excuse me, but did you tell Flo, she can walk through the woods all by herself?"

"I did."

"Zach. She's five."

"What are you scared of. She might get mauled by one of the deer?"

I cross my arms. "Very funny. What if she falls and hurts herself?"

He leaves the stove, comes up to me, and wraps his strong, warm arms around me. "How many times do I have to tell you, my little Scarlett? We are in paradise, and in paradise nothing bad can happen."

"Zach, you know—"

He swoops down and steals the words right out of my mouth.

When he lifts his head, I continue. "I still don't think she should be—"

He bends his head again. This time he slips his tongue between my lips. Something inside me melts. What the hell am I doing? It's my mom's birthday. Everything is perfect. There's no need to be over-protective. The woods are not dangerous. I've been playing there all my life.

He lifts his head and looks into my eyes.

"You're right," I whisper weakly.

"That's better." He grins. "I thought I was going to have to kiss you again. Which reminds me I didn't get to taste you this morning."

"Don't worry. You can do that tonight," I murmur.

"Oh, I intend to. Prepare to be eaten out for a *very* long time," he warns wolfishly.

"Oh, that's making me cream," I tease.

His eyes glint. "Are you trying to provoke me, Mrs. Black?"

"Maybe."

"Can both you stop kissing and whispering, please?" Florence asks impatiently next to us. She looks unbearably cute with her hand on her hips.

Zach laughs as we break apart. One day, young lady, you will have a man, then I will be come to your house, and stop you from kissing him."

"I'll lock the door," Florence shoots back.

"I'll blow down the door," Zach roars.

Florence starts laughing uproariously. "Like the bad wolf?"

"Like the bad wolf," Zach agrees

"Where's Brandon?" I ask.

"I'm in the toilet doing a very big poo, Mommy," my son screams from the downstairs toilet.

I look at Zach. "I thought you said nothing bad can happen in paradise?"

"Brandon's very big poo notwithstanding," he concedes, bending down to pick up Flo and swing her around.

Laughing, I walk towards the stove. I can see smoke coming from the pan. There's Brandon's very big poo, and there is a burnt pancake to contend with, but it's paradise for sure.

The End

COMING NEXT...

SAMPLE CHAPTER

PRETEND YOU'RE MINE

Dane

"Oh man, I'm so tanked," Robert says, running his hand through his sandy hair.

I'm pretty gone too. It's been so many years since Robert and I got drunk together. He used to be my best friend back in Blue Rock, before I moved to the city and became a workaholic. It's paid off big time, but sometimes, like now, I feel as if I've missed out on real life. Other people are getting married, having kids, and all I do is just make more and more money.

"Want to call it a night?" I ask.

He pours us both another whiskey. "Nah. I don't know when I'll get to drink with you again. I don't wanna sleep until I can't take it no more."

I lift the glass to my lips and knock half of it back while I study Robert over the rim. For a man who is getting married in two-weeks time, Robert doesn't look too happy. The more drunk he becomes the more morose he seems. I put my glass down and catch him looking at me. "What's up, Rob?"

He shrugs. "I was just wondering, you know."

I look at him curiously. "No. What?"

He sighs heavily. "Nah, forget it."

"Spit it out, man. You look like you're about to choke on it."

He straightens his spine and looks me dead in the eye. "What was it like when you were with Catherine?"

My eyes nearly pop out of my head. Where the hell did that come from? Catherine and I are ancient history. I can barely remember what she looked like. I might not even recognize her if I saw her again.

"Well?" he prompts.

I frown. "I don't know. That was so long ago, Rob. We were just kids."

"But what was she like? I mean, was she loving, aloof, clingy?"

I stare at him. "What's this about, Rob?"

"I'm just asking," he says defensively.

"Asking what exactly?"

He drops his head into his palms.

"What's going on Rob?"

He lifts his head and stares at me sadly. "I think Catherine is still in love with you."

"What?" I sputter in disbelief,

"It's true, Dane. I've tried to pretend it's not true, but I'm not a fool. I know she still has…feelings for you."

"You're wrong. We had nothing. It was just sex."

He winces as if it pains him to think of Catherine and me having sex.

"Listen, Rob. I assure you that it was just a passing thing. It meant nothing for either of us."

He stares at me intently. "So you feel nothing for her?"

"Hell, no."

"Not even a bit?"

I shake my head so vigorously it starts up a throbbing pain. "Look. I don't know where you got the idea she still has feelings for me from, but it can't be right. We haven't even spoken to each other since I left Blue Rock."

"She keeps asking about you, though," he insists miserably.

I frown. We had a great meal together and this is not at all how I envisaged the night ending.

"I'm worried she only got with me to keep close to you," he adds. "And I'm worried that when she sees you again, I mean look at you, she might leave me at the altar for you."

My jaw drops. "Jesus, Rob. What the fuck are you talking about?"

At that point, he holds his head in hands and starts sobbing. "Promise me, you won't run off with her, man. Please, Dane. I love her so much. She's the only woman I ever wanted. I loved even when she was your girl. I'd give anything up for her. Heck I'd die for that woman." He looks up at me. "Promise me, man. You won't tempt her. You won't flirt with her for old time sake, and you won't get too friendly with her. I hate to ask you this, but I'm desperate. I stood back last time and watched you have her, but it's my turn. I'm the one who is going to be there for her when she gets old and no one else wants her."

I stare at him in shock. I never realized he had been carrying such a soul-destroying idea all this while. All that time I was with her I never knew he was in love with her. To think of him suffering all this time with the thought that the woman he was crazy about and wanted to marry was still in love with me.

"God, if only you were married and you had a wife you could bring along. Then she'd know you were off limits. Shit. I can't believe I'm saying this to you."

"I have a fiancée...if that would help," I hear myself saying.

"What?" he asks, his eyes lighting up. "How come you never mentioned it before."

I feel a little sick to my stomach. It's been a long time since I've drunk this much. "Yeah, I was going to tell you about her."

"That's wonderful news, man."

I swallow hard. "Yeah. Wonderful."

"So when's the big day?"

"Oh, not for some time yet."

"But still. That's amazing, Dane. You'll bring her along to the wedding, won't you?"

"Of course."

"Has she met the family yet?"

"Not yet." I break a smile. "I'm trying to keep her to myself for as long as possible."

"I totally understand." He grins at me, but his cheeks are still wet with tears. "You know, all those things I said, you won't repeat them to anyone else, will you?"

"What things?"

"Thanks, man." He stands up, sways, then grins again at me. "I guess I better crash. I don't want to sick on the plane"

"Good idea. I have an early meeting tomorrow so I won't wake you, but I'll call you later in the day."

He nods and lurches towards the staircase. He stops at the bottom step, clutches the banister, and turns around to look at me. For a second, he looks like the old Rob, I knew. Swinging off tires and jumping into freezing cold rivers. Then the moment passes. "Thanks, Dane. I really appreciate what you're doing for me."

I smile back. "What's a best friend for?"

I stand and watch as he unsteadily makes his way up the stairs towards my guest bedroom. Then I go into my study, walk around the desk, and drop into my chair. Lifting my legs off the floor I swivel in my chair to face the window. The garden is in darkness, but I can see the glint of the Roman statue standing in the middle of the lake. I exhale the breath I've been holding.

Shit. Looks like I need to find myself a fake fiancée.

To be continued…

ABOUT THE AUTHOR

Thank you so much for reading!
Please click on the link below to receive info about my latest
releases and giveaways.
<u>NEVER MISS A THING</u>

Or
come and say hello here: